Praise for Joely Sue Burkhart's *Yours to Take*

"With concrete world building, multi-layered characters and a dynamic plot, this story is an excellent portrayal of a woman taking her first steps into the world of BDSM and struggling to hold onto the two men who have stolen her heart. Readers will be swept up in this emotional, extremely passionate tale and root for this threesome every step of the way."

~ *RT Book Reviews*

"I simply can't recommend this book highly enough, it's that good... [I'm] very pleased to give *Yours to Take* a 5 star rating."

~ *Guilty Pleasures Book Reviews*

"*Yours to Take* is a scintillating tale about pushing boundaries and finding love."

~ *Joyfully Reviewed*

"Ms. Burkhart did a splendid job adding emotion and heat to the story that not only had me eagerly turning the digital page for more, but also has my yearning for the next story in the *Connaghers* saga."

~ *Fallen Angel Reviews*

Look for these titles by
Joely Sue Burkhart

Now Available:

The Connaghers
Dear Sir, I'm Yours
Hurt Me So Good
Yours to Take

A Jane Austen Space Opera
Lady Doctor Wyre

Yours to Take

Joely Sue Burkhart

SAMHAIN
PUBLISHING

Samhain Publishing, Ltd.
11821 Mason Montgomery Road, 4B
Cincinnati, OH 45249
www.samhainpublishing.com

Editing by Tera Kleinfelter
Cover by Scott Carpenter

First Samhain Publishing, Ltd. electronic publication: May 2012
First Samhain Publishing, Ltd. print publication: April 2013

Dedication

For my beloved sister

A special thank you to Diana Castle for always meeting me Dark & Early; my editor extraordinaire, Tera Kleinfelter; and my tireless beta readers Sherri Meyer, Shannon Collins, Stephanie Christine, Willa Edwards, Nicole Tom, and Sharon Muha.

Chapter One

It didn't snow very often in Dallas, Texas, but when it did, everything came to a halt. Vicki Connagher paused at the deserted intersection. Shivering, she drew her coat tighter with her free hand. What a stupid idea. Since the store was only three blocks away, she'd thought she could get back with a few groceries before the storm hit. In just a matter of minutes, though, the sidewalks were already coated with ice.

Just one more block, she told herself, trudging across the slushy road. Snow still fell, thick and wet, dulling the usual noises of the city. Hot cocoa was going to taste especially good tonight. She'd bundle up on the couch in her favorite quilt and stay up all night watching cheesy horror movies. *Sounds like a blast, if I wasn't alone.*

But she was miserably alone. She'd end up working downstairs all night to avoid the emptiness of her apartment. Besides, she still had to come up with one more evening gown design before the gala. Since her mood was about as cheery as the Black Plague, she was going to need all the time she could get.

Her foot slid out and she fell with a curse. Getting wetter and colder by the minute, she muttered, "Not even chocolate is worth getting out in a freak Texas blizzard."

"Are you all right?"

The male voice startled her. Her heart slammed up into her throat and she whirled around, fumbling to get her keys gripped like claws between her fingers.

Hovering a safe distance away, the man held up both his hands in a non-threatening manner. With the streetlight shining down on his face, she recognized Jesse, a street artist she'd gotten to know during her law office days at Wagner & Leeman.

Seeing him brought back all the turmoil and grief that had driven her to quit her dream job.

It'd started innocently enough. Every time she was over by the park for lunch, she'd stop by his favorite bench beneath the largest tree. Handsome despite the grime, he always managed to make her smile, and she loved his work. She'd bought several of his charcoals and dropped a few bucks in his hat. Over the next few months, they'd talked, at first casually, but then as the stress of her job started to get to her, she found herself talking to him almost every day. She couldn't get through a day at court if she didn't take a lunch in the park. With Jesse.

Even her friends at the office had taken note of her "sponsorship" of the handsome young artist. It shamed her to remember how their jokes had embarrassed her. She'd cut back on those trips to the park, although she'd never been able to stay away for long. When she heard the horrible news that one of her clients had gunned down a policeman, she'd run to the park. Jesse had been there for her in a way that no one else had ever been in her entire life.

Jesse was the only person who'd ever seen her completely break down. Sobbing and sick with grief, she'd gone to him for comfort, and then to her great shame, she'd never gone back to see him again. She'd been too embarrassed that she'd let him in so deeply, a man she barely knew. A homeless man.

Cut to the core by her shallowness, she met his gaze and hoped he didn't hate her. "I'm fine. Nothing hurt but my pride. How are you, Jesse?"

"Good." He flashed a smile—revealing killer dimples—and helped her pick up the canned beans that had escaped her bag. "Haven't seen you around the park in a while."

Not even his ragged clothes could detract from that wholesome, down-to-earth smile and face. It'd been impossible not to like him from the start. "I quit my job and started my own business. Corporate life got to be too much for me."

He handed her the last can and then shyly pulled a small square out of his bag. "I made something for you."

When he didn't bring up that awful day in the park that had driven her to quit her job, she wanted to hug him. He didn't question or press her for answers. *No, he made me something, instead of accusing me of turning my back on him like so many other people must have.*

Blinking back tears because she hated to cry more than anything else, she held the folded paper up to the streetlight. On the front, he'd used watercolors to paint dozens of butterflies, laid on top of each other in carefully detailed layers so the entire page was covered in wings. Inside, he'd written a simple message: *Happy birthday, Vicki.*

"Sorry, I know your birthday was months ago, but I didn't know where you'd gone."

She tried to swallow the lump in her throat. "Oh, Jesse, thank you. How did you know?"

Shrugging self-consciously, he shifted the strap of his bag higher on his shoulder. "One of the last few times you stopped by, I overheard you tell your friend that you were planning a special dinner with your family for your birthday. I didn't mean to eavesdrop. Anyway, I've got a few new pieces you might like. Come over to the park when you get the chance."

"I will." She stared down at the card, thinking about how many weeks he'd carried it in his bag, protecting it from getting torn or dirty, hoping to see her. He'd made her a card, when some of her best friends hadn't remembered her birthday at all. She'd lost more than her career. "Thank you, Jesse. This really means a lot to me."

He tipped his battered, lopsided straw hat, gave her another gorgeous smile that seemed so out of place on a homeless man's face, and turned to head down the street. Alone. His skinny shoulders hunched against the cold.

Vicki had built in her mind all sorts of reasons of why he was on the streets, but she'd never had the courage to ask him. He only had on a jean jacket, no gloves, and the knapsack tossed over his shoulder, exactly how she'd seen him countless times. Everything he owned in the world must be in that bag.

"Jesse?"

Immediately, he turned around and came back toward her, his eyes wide and hopeful. It was too dark to make out the remarkable turquoise shade of his eyes, but she remembered. "Yes, ma'am?"

"Do you have someplace to go?"

"Oh, sure." He nodded, but she didn't like the way he ducked his head. "Don't worry about me. Come over to the park when you get the chance. I miss seeing you."

She took the last few steps toward her building, her mind screaming all the reasons it would be stupid to ask him inside. She was alone. He was a man, bigger and stronger than her even if she had a few years on him. She had a damned good security system on both the shop and her apartment upstairs, but if he chose to overpower her, she wouldn't have a chance to call for help.

She didn't really know him at all. A few lunches in the park, a couple of hours of casual talking, and one time she'd needed a non-judgmental friend. He was homeless, for God's sake, and had probably seen more crime and violence than she'd even dreamed of despite working all those years as a defense attorney. But there was something undeniable in his eyes, a deep, soul-piercing light that she couldn't forget. Without saying a word, he managed to reach inside her and tug, hard, amplifying her guilt and worry.

It wasn't her fault that he was homeless, but it would be her fault if he froze to death tonight. *I refuse to turn my back on him ever again.*

Putting on her best formidable, cast-iron face that had intimidated many a shady character into providing better testimony, she turned and faced him squarely. "If you promise to behave yourself, you can come home with me tonight."

His eyes flared with horror and he recoiled a step, which instantly made her feel better about asking him. His mouth opened, but it took him several times before he could say anything. "Oh, no, ma'am. That wouldn't be right. I just wanted to make sure you were okay—it didn't even occur to me that you might... No, please, I couldn't."

"I couldn't sleep a wink if you were freezing out here all night." She opened the door to the shop and flipped on the light. He hovered behind her, staring at the warmth and shelter longingly. "I'm making a huge batch of chili and cornbread."

His shoulders shook, but he didn't move closer.

"What I really wanted was hot cocoa. That's why I went out tonight before the weather got too horrible. Not cocoa from a mix or powder—I want the real thing. I'm going to make some first."

"With real milk?" His voice sounded hoarse. He took a step closer, but kept his shoulders down, hunched, as though he were trying to make himself smaller and less threatening. "And marshmallows?"

"Real milk, real chocolate," she promised. "But I don't have marshmallows. I think they're disgusting. Come on in, Jesse. I'm not the world's greatest cook, but I can make a mean pot of beans."

He hung his head, one hand gripping the strap of his bag so hard his knuckles were white. "I've been in trouble before, ma'am, but I haven't been arrested in more than five years, and I've been clean since. Call one of your old contacts in the police department and check up on me."

She was surprised at his willingness to share his unsavory past—and a little disconcerted that he knew so much about her. "I can do that. I should also warn you that my very mean and much bigger, older brother could be here in minutes."

Leading the way through the long tables stacked with fabrics and trim, she flipped on another light. *Now I know why my security guy insisted I have a separate system for my upstairs apartment.* "I set up this place so that my seamstress could sleep over when we're on a time crunch. There's a bed, clean linen and a full-sized bathroom."

Jesse risked a quick glance at the room but otherwise kept his head down, his shoulders so tight that he was as short as her, when he was actually several inches taller. Lightly, she touched his arm. He flinched, but at least his head came up. She was struck again by the intensity of his eyes, so clear and honest despite the harshness of his life.

"Are you sure?" His voice shook. "I didn't mean—"

"I'm sure." She smiled, gently squeezing his arm. He was so thin, just bones and tight, wiry muscle lay over the top. "Look around on the shelves in the closet—I think I stuck some of my brother's old clothes in there. Take a shower and come upstairs when you're done. I'll have the cocoa ready in no time."

"My full name is Jesse Dean Inglemarre and I'm twenty-five. Check me out. If you're not comfortable, tell me to leave. I swear on a stack of Bibles that I'll leave immediately, no questions asked. I won't ever bother you again."

He was several years older than she'd guessed, although still several years younger than her. She smiled to put him at ease. It felt right, so very, very right, to help him. "You're not bothering me."

Solemnly, he stared into her eyes, searching her face, even though he didn't ask, *Why me? Why are you doing this?*

How could she explain it? Sometimes after a particularly bad trial, the only bright spot in her day had been walking through the park to see what new drawing he might be working on. Once he'd smiled at her, she'd found the courage to trudge back to work. On this cold, lonely night he was a welcome surprise. "There's something about you, Jesse."

Oh, there's something about me all right, Jesse thought sadly, waiting until she shut the door before looking about the room. Simple, spartan, and the most glorious thing he'd seen in years, until he found a stack of clean clothes on the shelf. Even musty from storage, they smelled like heaven. Then he saw the shampoo and soap in the bathroom, and he found himself crying beneath the steaming hot water.

God, so incredible. People didn't know what a luxury it could be simply to be clean. To have a spare set of clean clothes. To be in a safe enough place to risk taking off his filthy clothes and washing completely. Bliss. Pure bliss.

It all came from the most gorgeous, unforgettable woman he'd ever met. He had no pride left, or surely he'd be ashamed that he'd come to her like this and she'd taken him in like an abandoned puppy. He'd depended on seeing her every day, but then she'd quit coming to the park. She'd given him one taste of heaven and then disappeared off the face of the earth.

He hadn't even known her full name or where she worked. One of the women he'd seen her with occasionally had dropped the fact that Vicki had left the firm to start her own business down by Oak Lawn. So he'd started hanging out in this neighborhood, hoping to find her.

Never in a million years had he thought she'd let him inside her home. All he'd wanted to do was see her again, find her place, and maybe stop by once a week or so, just to talk. Just to see her smile at his latest work.

I know where to find her now. He scrubbed his hair a second time. *I can't stay long. She's sheltering me from the cold, that's all.*

She has no idea that I'm hopelessly in love with her.

Vicki dialed the number and laid the phone down on the counter in speaker mode. Chopping chocolate, she counted the rings. Mentally, she rearranged her questions in the most logical order that would lead to the best possible outcome with the least amount of suspicion.

"Reyes."

By the sharp bark of Elias's voice, she knew he was already frustrated. Hell, he was always frustrated. Working on a narcotics task force overwhelmed by the Mexican drug cartels tended to frustrate even the most patient of men. A lot could be said about Elias Reyes, but he wasn't exactly patient.

She decided to be professional and not friendly. He hadn't been by in months, and she couldn't remember the last time they'd had sex. Okay, that was a lie; she'd never forget a moment with Elias, even though they'd fought constantly about their jobs. Then his partner had been killed by one of her old clients in a drug bust gone bad. He still hadn't forgiven her, and she'd found herself sobbing in the arms of a homeless man in the park instead of her lover's.

Now that she'd started her own business, she was still too busy, and he certainly hadn't bothered to come by. "I need you to run a name through your database."

"Vik," he drawled out his nickname for her in that low, sexy voice that always made her want to throw her head back and moan deep in her throat. "I thought you quit defending assholes I put away."

"I did." She refused to allow her tone to sharpen defensively. "I need a background run on somebody and you're the only person in the Dallas PD who'll still take my calls."

He let out a low grunt of agreement. "What's the name?"

"Jesse Dean Inglemarre."

"What exactly are you looking for?"

She heard him typing. He must be at work and already looking up the data for her. Who was she kidding—Elias was always at work. "Any warrants, recent arrests, known gang affiliation. Standard stuff."

"Got a soc?"

"Nope, but I know he's twenty-five years old."

A few moments went by. She didn't hear any voices. Usually his office was loud and rowdy at any hour. The war on drugs never slept.

"Looks like your boy last got in trouble five years ago, but nothing recent. No known address. How do you know him?"

"He's a street artist." She tried to keep her tone casual and strictly to the truth. Elias could sniff out a lie quicker than a bloodhound. "I used to see him when I worked at Wagner & Leeman. Thanks, Elias. I hope you're not out in this snow tonight."

"Not so fast, Vik."

Mentally, she groaned. He always was too damned smart for his own good, which meant he was a fine cop who always suspected the worst in people. Unfortunately, he was almost always right.

"Why the sudden interest in a homeless street artist in the middle of a snow storm? Surely you're not thinking about letting this punk into your home."

"Thanks," she said firmly. "I'll talk to you later."

"Fuck." In her mind, she could see him at his desk, jumping to his feet and raking his hand through his hair. "You did. You invited this asshole into your home. Are you insane? He's a druggie. A scumbag. You know they can never come clean. Give them a ten and they'll buy a hit instead of food."

"He's not like that." She used her softest voice, trying to calm him down before he decided to get on his white horse and charge over here like a knight in shining armor. "He just needs a little help."

"Jesus, Vik, does he have any weapons? Did he bring drugs into your house?"

"No!" *Although I didn't think to check.* "I can handle this, Reyes." Deliberately, she emphasized his cop name, the cold and formal relationship they'd used at their jobs even when they shared a bed once in a while. "I don't want you to interfere."

"You should have thought of that before you invited a homeless junkie to spend the night!"

"I have my phone right here and you're on speed dial. I promise I'll call you if I get even a hint of a weird vibe from him, but he's barely more than a kid, Elias. He's not going to hurt me."

"You're damned right he's not."

"What the hell does that mean?"

"He's not a kid, Vik, even if he looks helpless and innocent to you. He hasn't been a kid in a long time. One of his raps was for prostitution when he was barely sixteen. Yeah, he must be a real pretty boy, huh? I'm surprised he came on to you. Seems like a rich queer is more up his alley."

The thought of Jesse's brilliant eyes scrunched up with pain or staring up at a jerk forcing him to give a blowjob made her knees quiver hard enough that she had to sit on a barstool. She'd known he must have had a hard life, but the reality made her stomach heave. "He didn't come on to me."

"Maybe he'll come on to me, then."

"He's not like that." Her voice quivered, betraying her. She clenched her jaws a moment, concentrating on retrieving that calm, cool exterior she'd learned as a defense attorney. "I saw him in the snow and cold—he was helping me because I fell on the ice!—and I couldn't leave him out there."

"If you used to see him over at the park near Wagner & Leeman, then why the hell was he way out by your place? He was staking you out, Vik. He knew exactly what he was doing

19

when he just happened to walk by. I bet he seemed real shocked to find you, didn't he? They're damned good actors when they need to be."

Torn between outrage and concern, she tried to remember if she'd ever told Jesse where she lived. Would he really come dozens of blocks in the cold to give her a birthday card? Surely, he couldn't have pretended that much surprise when she asked him to come inside. She was a good judge of character. She'd seen more than her share of bad guys willing to sell their mamas if it would get them out of prison.

"Jesse's not like that. He's not one of the bad guys, Elias. I can see it in his eyes. He needs someone to give him a break."

Wheels screeched on the street below so loudly that she jumped up and ran to the window. Elias jumped out of his truck and stormed up to the door of her building. "I'll give him a break. I'll break his fucking arm if he even lays a finger on you."

She glared down at him, whether he could actually see her or not. "I told you I could handle this!"

"Let me in, Vik, or I'm going to owe you a new door."

Elias heard her shouting at him as she ran down the stairs, but he didn't stop. He threw open the door to the rear living quarters, grabbed the invader, and slammed him face-first against the wall with a satisfying crunch.

The kid didn't put up a fight. *Man*, Elias reminded himself. Not a kid, no matter how scrawny and slender he was, not at twenty-five years of age.

Vicki screamed, a high, shrill wail like nothing he'd ever heard from her. "Jesse!"

Her terrified voice pierced through Elias's rage. As a kid huddled in a narrow bed with his younger brothers and sisters while his crazy father beat the shit out of his mother, he'd sworn to never make a woman scream like that. He slapped cuffs on the man and forced himself to ease off. He had to be the cop in this, not the enraged, jealous, overprotective—and almost always absent—lover.

The junkie stayed against the wall, legs automatically spread. He knew the drill all too well.

"You don't smell like a bum, so I guess you've already taken advantage of your hostess's hot water. Do you have anything stashed in these nice clean pockets?"

"No, sir."

Damn it, he even sounded like a kid, his voice breathless and shaking with fear. Elias twisted his lips into a furious snarl. The punk was afraid of being caught. Afraid of being thrown in jail instead of enjoying a nice cushy night under Vicki's roof, stealing everything not locked down while she slept.

She stepped between them, her face white and her mouth tight with strain. "I gave him those pants. How dare you come in here and throw him around like this? He's hurt! Look at him, Elias, he's bleeding!"

Crying, she cradled the jerk's face in her hands and wiped the blood from his split lip with a tissue snatched from the bedside table. "Jesse, I'm so sorry. I didn't know he'd come over like this. I didn't know he'd hurt you."

"It's okay. He's protecting you. I've had much worse done to me."

The nicer he acted—pretended to be!—the worse Elias felt, which pissed him off even more. He grabbed the ratty duffel bag lying at the foot of the bed and dumped it out, using an ink pen to separate items so he didn't get poked by a dirty needle. "Any weapons? Drugs? Paraphernalia?"

"No, sir. Just my straight-edge razor. I've used it as protection a few times, but no knives or guns. I haven't touched drugs in five years. I'll take a drug test right this minute if you order it."

Elias flipped open a small wooden case, but all it contained was tiny whittled down pencils and precious little nubs of chalk, so used up that a normal person—with money—would have thrown them out and replaced them long ago. Feeling more and more like a heel, he methodically emptied the pockets of everything. Wadded up small bills littered the bed. A five in each denim pocket, a twenty in the threadbare shirt, several more bills tucked into the rolled socks, but certainly no nice wad of cash that a dealer would carry. Spreading the bills out across the meager belongings would make it more difficult to steal his precious savings.

"I have a hundred dollar bill in each boot hidden beneath the insole." Jesse leaned against the wall as though the entire building would crumble around them without his weight propping it up. The pants sagged low on his slim hips, and he didn't have on a shirt. Bones moved beneath his skin in sharp, painful relief. The kid was half-starved and malnourished. In despair, he hung his head, his streaked golden-brown hair falling down to hide his face. "Took me a year to save that much because the punks on the street keep stealing it. They know I don't have a weapon."

Elias knew the answer, but he wanted to see how many lies the kid might weave. "How do you know Vicki?"

"She used to come to Highland Park where I hang out. When she quit coming, I asked one of her friends what had happened. I missed her, and I wanted to make sure she was okay. She was always nice to me, but I never thought she'd help me like this."

"Get these cuffs off him," Vicki said in a deceptively pleasant voice that sent shards of ice skittering down his spine. This was the defense attorney, not a woman who'd called him to check out a friend. "He answered your questions satisfactorily and you have nothing to charge him with. He's not trespassing and he's not a danger to me or himself."

When he hesitated, she narrowed those glittering dark eyes on him and lowered her chin, preparing for the charge. "I might not work for Leeman any longer, but I'll have him crawling in every orifice you've got unless you release Jesse immediately."

Chapter Two

Uneasy and tense with the other man sitting beside him at the breakfast bar, Jesse took a sip of the cocoa she'd made and all his nerves simply melted away. Vicki hid a smile behind her cup.

Even Elias's mood seemed to sweeten with each sip of chocolaty warm goodness, although he grumbled as she poured fresh coffee into her mug. "Why you insist on ruining good hot chocolate with coffee is beyond me."

"I don't understand how you can work twenty-hour days without spiking your drink with extra caffeine every chance you get. If you two can enjoy your cocoa without killing each other, I need to start the cornbread."

Jesse peeked up at her, a quick, furtive glance through his tumbled hair. He'd always worn it pulled back in a ponytail. She'd never realized that his hair was more blond than brown. All tumbled and loose about his face, his hair set his stunning turquoise eyes off to perfection. With his full, luscious lips and strong jaw, he could have been a GQ model, not a homeless junkie selling himself on the street corner.

What happened to you, Jesse?

Blinking back tears, she retrieved the eggs and milk from the fridge and the cornmeal from the pantry. When she lugged out the iron skillet and melted butter, Elias dared a question. "Don't you use a mix?"

"Hell no," she retorted in mock outrage. "No Southerner worth her salt would serve cornbread made out of a box or cook it in anything but an iron skillet. You can't get the nice crusty edges without it, and the box mixes are too sweet."

"I suppose you don't put ketchup in your chili either."

She pressed her hand to her heart and pretended faintness. "Never. Surely I've made chili for you before, haven't I? Good Texas chili should be more meat than beans, with a beer thrown in for good measure."

Shutting the oven door on the batter-filled skillet, she straightened and caught a look on Jesse's face that knocked her back on her heels. A bit of accusation, followed by resignation. Maybe she hadn't been hard enough on Elias after he'd busted in like a crazed jerk. *Or maybe my young friend harbors feelings for me that I never allowed myself to consider.*

She swallowed hard at the memory of Jesse's arms around her, his low murmurs in her ear while she'd sobbed like a baby.

Jesse studied the bottom of his cup like he was surprised he'd found it so quickly. "How long have you known each other?"

Taking the hint, she poured him another cup of cocoa. "Oh, let's see. I worked at Wagner & Leeman about seven years, counting my time as an intern. How long have you been on the DPD, Detective Reyes?"

"Fifteen years," Elias replied, his mouth down turned in a frown. "Long, hard years, especially when dealing with an annoyingly talented defense attorney who managed to get off just about every drug dealer in the city."

She turned back to the stove and kept her mouth shut. She refused to give him the pleasure of arguing yet again, but she dumped in more—a lot more—cayenne pepper. She loved spicy chili, but Elias would probably be up all night moaning about his stomach.

"I still didn't really know Vik until the last year or so. Some weeks she tolerates me more than others."

Which was a piss-poor way of saying they were off again, on again lovers, whenever he could drag himself away from those drug dealers he blamed her for being back out on the street. Even though she'd quit the firm months ago.

"How long have you been on the street?"

She couldn't help but stiffen with interest and alarm both, although she didn't turn around to see how Jesse took the other man's question. Long moments went by before he answered.

"I left home when I was fifteen, a proud, stupid kid who thought I knew better than my old man. He was a washed-up, wannabe country singer doing bars in Nashville, trying to catch a break, and I thought he was a mean bastard. I hung with the wrong crowd, made some bad decisions, dropped out of school, got arrested for shoplifting, drugs, you name it."

Vicki turned so she could see his face. He smiled, a strange, beautiful twist of his mouth that made her want to cry for him.

He dropped his gaze to his hands wrapped around his cup. "When you're young and stupid, you don't think the bad stuff could ever possibly happen to you. You can drink and drive and not get caught, certainly never wreck your car or hurt anyone else. You can go to class or your job high and no one will ever know. You can walk out on your old man, call him every name in the book, and laugh when you find out the mean SOB died of a heart attack. Then you realize that you were the only one stupid enough to buy your bullshit, and the only person left in the whole world who ever cared about you is gone."

She couldn't help but take his trembling hand in hers. He clung to her but didn't look up.

"I've done bad things. I've seen and lived worse. I've tried to leave those things behind, but they aren't as easy to wash off as the dirt."

"There are shelters..." Elias began in a gentle voice, but Jesse only shook his head on a harsh laugh.

"I'd rather go back to prison. At least then I'd know the man raping me would protect me in the yard tomorrow." He raised his head, his eyes pleading for understanding. "When I got out of prison, I was clean and I'd earned my GED while behind bars. I had two minimum-wage jobs and I gladly worked my ass off. I had an apartment—wasn't much and I paid by the week, but it was mine. I could lock the door and sleep almost through the night without waking up, terrified that someone was coming in.

"But then I got sick. Just the flu, but as soon as I missed a day of work, they fired me. I didn't have much money saved, and I lost my apartment as soon as I missed the first week's rent. I didn't have any place to go, no family left, no one to take me in but the drug dealers I'd known before jail.

"I could have gone back to running drugs for them, selling on the corners and in the schools, but I didn't. It would have been a hell of a lot easier. I live on what I earn with my art, drug-free and legal, but once you lose everything, it's hard to get people to see you. If I walk in for an interview in the only decent pair of jeans I've got left, it won't matter if I shaved or if my fingernails are clean, because I still stink of the streets."

Vicki didn't realize she was crying until Elias slipped an arm around her shoulders and drew her against him. Jesse

27

loosened his fingers on her hand, but she gripped him tighter, refusing to let him go. "See?" She buried her face against Elias's shirt, hating for anyone to see her so vulnerable. "See why I had to help him?"

"I know," he whispered, rocking her gently. "You were right. I apologize, Jesse, for slamming you up against the wall like that. I should have trusted her judgment."

"You saw me. *Me*," Jesse whispered, but his voice rang with intent. "You've already given me a chance to get a real job by letting me take a shower. I look like a normal, decent person, someone who can get a job, and for that, I can't thank you enough."

"You're going to stay here." Wiping her eyes, Vicki straightened and shot a firm glare at Elias, silencing whatever arguments he might throw at her. "I'll help you find a job and get back on your feet. No matter how long it takes, you won't end up on the street again. Do you hear me?"

A ghost of a smile flickered on Jesse's lips and he ducked his head, as though tipping his hat to her. "Yes'm."

"If something happens to you again, if you're ever out there, lost, alone, then you call *me*." Her voice broke but she didn't soften her stance. She leaned across the counter, squeezing his hand to make sure he met her gaze. "Call me. Anytime. Anywhere. Reverse the charges. Mail me a letter. Whatever it takes. I'll come get you and bring you home. You can count on me to be there for you."

His eyes gleamed with unshed tears, crystal jewels in spring water. "You...I..." He bowed his head, shoulders shaking. His tears fell on the back of her hand still gripping his. Raggedly, he whispered, "I've never had a real home."

"You can always come home to me."

Elias had never seen Vicki's nurturing side, not like this. Bemused, he watched her stuff the kid full of chili and cornbread until he could barely keep his eyes open. She practically tucked him into bed, making sure he had a dozen blankets before sending him downstairs. "If you need anything, just buzz the door. I'm going to arm the security system on the entire building before I head to bed."

Mumbling his thanks, Jesse headed down the stairs to the lower apartment. When he paused and looked back up at her like she was the most beautiful angel he'd ever seen in his life, Elias put his arm around her and drew her into his side.

"Good night, Jesse," he said firmly, staking his claim on her. "We'll see you in the morning."

Shrugging off his arm, she pulled away and shut the door. "That was cruel."

"He needs to know that you're taken."

"By who?" She marched into the kitchen and attacked the dishes like they'd shot her mama. Elias had met Mrs. Connagher, and that would be a feat indeed. "I haven't seen you in at least three months. If I hadn't called you tonight..."

"I was on my way over." He refused to admit just how many nights he'd been sitting outside her apartment, keeping watch, supposedly, but mostly trying to convince his pride to bend just a little. "That's why I got here so fast."

"So now you're psychic? You felt the subtle forces of the universe warning that another male was encroaching on your territory?"

He loaded the dishwasher for her, although she kept rearranging things to her satisfaction. "You know how crazy my job is. I haven't slept in a week."

"I know," she said quietly, but her eyes snapped with dark fire. "I know that you have an important, demanding, extremely

29

dangerous job on which this entire city depends. I've never bitched about you being a cop and you know it."

"But—"

She threw up a hand holding a sudsy ladle and shook it at him like a weapon. "There's a difference between being dedicated to your job and totally neglecting the people who care about you. You haven't been *here*, spiritually or mentally, let alone physically, in months. You haven't called me. You haven't stopped by for a five-minute cup of coffee. You haven't given me a hug and kiss on your way downtown. You didn't even send me a card on my birthday."

He winced. *Damn, I knew I forgot something.*

"I've been going through a major, life-changing event alone without even a warm body to hold on to at night, a trusted ear to whisper my fears and doubts, a shoulder to cry on. I quit my job, left all my friends and my career, to open up my own business. I'm putting in as many hours as you so I can launch my line next month. You can't be bothered to even stop by for a quickie in between jailing bad guys, but a homeless guy who barely knows my name worried enough about me to track me down simply to say hello in the worst storm in years. Oh, and he had a birthday card for me, one he'd made with his own hands. And what do you do? You bust open his mouth and threaten to break his arm."

"He could have hurt you, Vik. I was perfectly justified in searching his things."

"Sure." She nodded pleasantly and walked toward the bedroom, flipping off lights as she went except for a lamp in the living room. "But you didn't have to hurt him to make your point. It makes me sick to think about how many people have physically hurt him over the years, and the man I care about is now one of them."

Elias didn't want to piss her off, but he was determined to get the truth laid out. "He thinks he loves you. I saw the way he looked at you. Now that you're so determined to save him, he'll only love you more."

She rummaged in her closet and pulled out a stack of blankets and a pillow. "Why on earth would you think that?"

How many fucking blankets did the kid need? Damn it, seeing her bed, remembering the last time he'd held her, made him as hard as a rock. He'd been aching ever since he'd laid eyes on her tonight. Watching her pet that kid's hand and take such good care of him had only reminded him how long it'd been since he'd been on the receiving end of her affection.

"Are your spidey, super-cop senses blaring again? Because he still doesn't even know my full name. How could he possibly love me?"

"You're gorgeous, Vik, and too tenderhearted for your own good, even when you try to act mean and tough. How could he not love you?"

Facing him, she curved her lips into a slow, wide smile that made him think uncomfortably of sharks. "So if I'm following your argument, you must love me too. Right? Do you love me, Elias?"

His mouth went dry, his tongue swelled into a thick wad of cotton, and his stomach churned on that brutal chili she'd made. God, he hated it when she did that—leading him right into the trap she'd laid for him, just like he was on the stand and she needed to disprove his credibility.

His hackles rose. "Are you sure you don't have ice water running in your veins? No wonder those bastards at your law office loved you so much. Vicki Connagher can get anybody out of jail, no questions asked."

She shoved the blankets into his arms and slammed the bedroom door in his face. "I love you too, Elias."

You can always come home to me.

Jesse had never dared to let the dream play out in his mind, that she might take him into her home, family and life. That she'd fight for him, stand up to her boyfriend for his sake, or drop whatever she was doing and come help him, no matter where he might be. He'd thought it impossible for him to ever belong anywhere, let alone with—and to—her.

It wasn't her house or possessions that made him want to fall on his knees with thanksgiving. It was Vicki. She'd always been the center of his meager existence. Now, she'd taken him off the streets and protected him. She'd held his hand and sworn to help him.

That made *her* his home.

Staring up at the ceiling, he tried not to picture her lying in her bed with her boyfriend, but it was a losing battle. Maybe her bedroom was right above. If so, he'd be able to hear them making love. He'd hear her pleasure. The thought made him unbearably hard, his cock throbbing in the borrowed cotton pants, but he did nothing about it.

All his arousal was for her, if she wanted it. If she needed it. In his mind, he imagined her giving him the order not to touch himself. No pleasure unless she gave it.

She didn't wear a ring, so he didn't think she was that serious about the cop, but they'd obviously known each other a long time. They had a way of working together, even when they spat and clawed at each other like alley cats. Reyes made it painfully obvious that he'd claimed her. He wouldn't hesitate to throw anyone dumb enough to challenge him up against the wall again to protect what was his.

Jesse didn't care if the cop had primary claim on her, not really, as long as *she* claimed *him*. He'd do anything she wanted. Hell, he'd beg the cop to do him if that's what it took to stay close and eventually find his way to her—their—bed.

Claim me as yours, even if that means I have to be his.

Chapter Three

Vicki opened the door with a huge smile that was as much a wondrous luxury as the soft bed and warm blankets. "Morning, Jesse. How'd you sleep?"

"Great, thank you so much. I can't remember the last time I slept like that. Did I sleep too late?"

"Of course not. I don't plan to let you do anything but sleep and eat all day. You need the rest. Besides, the snow's so bad that everything's closed today. Elias called and said he barely made it downtown."

Relieved that the other man was long gone, Jesse stepped inside, enjoying the sweet smell of something baking and the welcoming, natural warmth of her home. He noted the folded blankets and pillow on the couch. She'd headed toward the kitchen, so she didn't see his fierce, glad smile at the thought of the cop stuck on the couch last night.

Good for her. Good for me.

"How do you take your coffee?" she called, her voice drawing him like the ceaseless power of the moon over the tides. "Take a seat. Breakfast's almost ready."

"Hot. Leaded. Anything else is a bonus."

She set a steaming mug in front of him along with a carton of cream. "There's sugar in the bowl if you want it."

"Can I help you with something?"

"Later," she promised as if she knew that he burned to pay her back in whatever way possible. "Let's figure out a game plan first. Like my oldest brother always says, you can't expect to win the game if you don't *plan* to win." Smiling softly, she cocked a hip against the bar and watched him spoon in sugar and cream. "You said last night that you have your GED. I know you're a talented artist. What else do you like to do? What can you do?"

He took a sip of coffee, reveling in the rich, strong taste on his tongue, while he carefully considered how best to respond. He'd never lie to her, but she might not accept—or believe—the truth, at least not before getting to know him better. "I'll do anything. Shovel manure. Load trucks. Wash dishes."

Let your cop slam me up against the wall again.

She frowned, and he was afraid he'd said that last bit out loud. "Maybe the better question would be, what do you want to avoid? You're too talented an artist to be stuck doing manual labor all your life."

"I don't mind. I'll always do the art in my free time."

"I'll call my brother and see if he has any positions open at VCONN. I trust him to take good care of you." The oven dinged, so she removed the pan of muffins. "Hope you like blueberries."

If this brother was the big, mean one she'd mentioned last night—and even half as powerful and charismatic as his sister—Jesse could only hope to survive the interview intact. "I'll eat anything."

She slid a saucer in front of him bearing a piping hot muffin that made his mouth water. His stomach rumbled like he'd never eaten a crumb of food in his life. Flushing, he dropped his gaze. It was all he could do not to fall on the food like a starving wolf.

Her hands closed over his and he jumped in his seat, jerking his gaze up to hers. She bowed her head. "Dear Father in heaven, thank you for bringing Jesse to me. Help me find him a good job, and forgive me for keeping this prayer short because I'm starving too. Amen."

She started to pull her hands back, but he couldn't help but twist his hands in her grip so he could clutch her fingers a moment. Staring into her dark chocolate eyes, he tried to convey his feelings without saying a word. Maybe it worked, because her eyes sparked and her fingers convulsed.

Gently, she pulled free. "More coffee?"

"No thank you, ma'am."

"Please don't call me that. You make me feel as old as my mother. My name is Vicki." Grimacing, she refilled her cup. "Well, that's not actually my real name. My oldest brother's name is Victor. When I was little, I couldn't say his name, but I could say V, and I liked him to call me Little V. Eventually, my family settled on calling me Vicki, much to my relief. My middle brother always told me I was lucky—at least they hadn't given me his name, Verrill."

Two brothers he'd have to deal with, on top of the cop. "Sounds like your family has a weird thing for names that begin with V."

"Oh, yeah, you could say that. Mama's name is Virginia, so my parents decided to name us all with V names. My real name's Beulah Virginia, after my Grandma too, but if you ever call me that, I'll be tempted to hogtie you."

His heart pounded, his palms sweated, and he swayed. Struggling to regain control, he willed the image away. Bound, helpless, for her. God, he could die a very happy man if that ever happened.

"Jesse? Are you okay?"

Trying to hide how much she affected him, he took a mouthful of muffin. So sweet, so good, but not as good as that little fantasy she'd unintentionally given him. "I'm fine. Just hungry, ma'am."

"Vicki." She arched a brow at him in challenge. "And my last name is Connagher."

"Vicki." What a rush to be given her real name, along with the permission to use it. Luckily, she put another muffin on his plate. Eating seconds bought him enough time for his hard-on to ease.

Hours passed in companionable, comfortable silence. Jesse had a way of being present and close without being intrusive. When she headed downstairs to work on her designs, he automatically slipped into "work" mode and let her think without making her feel like she needed to entertain him.

However, her nagging problem wouldn't let her get any work done. She couldn't figure out what was wrong with her line and she was running out of time. "Something's missing."

He looked up from his own art. "Would it help to talk through your ideas?"

"Actually, it might. If you don't mind."

He'd already set his paper aside and stood to join her. "I'll never mind anything you ask."

The way he said it—his voice all low and fervent—made things tighten in her body that hadn't been interested in anybody but Elias in a very long time.

Maybe he's right to be jealous.

Shaken, she busied herself with shifting the racks to display each outfit clearly. She hadn't come to any sort of permanent relationship or agreement with him, but she cared for him. When she wasn't totally infuriated, she could admit that she loved him. Even though he'd been absent for three months, that didn't give her any reason to feel attracted to Jesse. He was so grateful for her help, God only knew how far he'd go out of a sense of obligation.

The thought made her hands tremble, that she could be capable of abusing him like that, one of countless people who'd hurt and used him.

I'm not going to take advantage of him just because I'm lonely and pissed at my boyfriend. He—and Elias too—deserves better than that.

"I need ten solid outfits for the show next month." Her voice quivered, but he didn't seem to notice. "They should all fit together seamlessly and tell a story. They don't have to use exactly the same colors or fabrics, but there should be a cohesiveness that brings the line together. Since I worked in a law office, I want to target professional women who need to move from the courtroom or office to an evening out with the least amount of fuss, with the occasional special outfit for big events."

She turned the first rack containing a red gown around so he could see the low-cut back. "Understated, but sexy. I designed this one for my soon-to-be sister-in-law. She's already worn it once to a charity event, but I'm still going to use it to open the show."

"I don't know much about fashion." Jesse fingered the silk, lifted the hem, and admired the way the skirt fluttered down. "The back is unique, low cut, but narrower than I would expect. Is that deliberate?"

She couldn't help the slow burn heating her cheeks. How to put it nicely without embarrassing herself? "The V-cut back is significant to her and my brother, and I had to make it narrower than usual to hide...er...the...marks. The bruises."

Jesse's eyes flared and he made a tiny noise.

"The bruises come from mutual agreement and enjoyment for them both, okay? My brother's a Master, a sadist, actually, and she loves him exactly the way he is. For that, I love her too, and I wanted to give her a gown that made a statement, that proclaimed her as belonging to him, but also provide them privacy because not everybody will understand. She wore it to a charity event last month and was absolutely stunning. She even wore his collar publicly. It was a huge step for my brother too."

"Do you understand?" Now it was Jesse's turn for his voice to quiver. Eyes soft as though he daydreamed, he stroked his fingers unconsciously on his throat. "I mean, you must, or you wouldn't have created such a meaningful gown just for her."

"I do, but I guess I try not to think about it." Vicki studied the dress, because that was easier than staring into his piercing eyes and feeling that pull again. She'd been afraid that he'd be creeped out by her family skeletons in the closet, but instead she might have accidentally turned him on. "My brother is heavily involved in the S&M community, and he invited me to come to events before. I don't know why he's expecting me to come, so I laugh and blow him off. God, I can't believe I'm telling you all this."

Instead of being offended, Jesse laughed softly. "I'm glad, Vicki. Everybody needs someone to talk to. Sometimes I missed that more than a roof over my head."

Lying awake at night, worrying about Elias out on the streets, getting shot at by drug runners, she'd known the horrors of loneliness. "I can," she whispered on a soft sigh. "These past few months have been hard, much harder than I imagined. I can't tell you how nice it is to have someone to bounce ideas off."

"So tell me about this one." Jesse shifted the conversation back to safer ground, for which she was extremely grateful.

She walked him through all the completed outfits, ranging in color from the red-silk gown to a sleek black pantsuit and a zebra-striped dress that she absolutely adored. Paired with a conservative black cashmere jacket, she would have worn it to the office without hesitation, but without the coat, it would have been perfect for dinner at any five-star restaurant.

"I think I see the problem." He stepped back to look at the outfits together. "Speaking as an artist, there's no softness in your color palette. You have brilliant red, pure white, and somber black. You have a few pieces in gray to help relieve the bolder colors, but overall it's so...so..."

"Conservative." She blew out her breath. "Yeah, I think I see what you mean."

"You need an accent, something that's a surprise. It doesn't have to be much. Just a touch of softness in an unexpected color."

"A new color." She mused out loud, tapping her finger against her lips. "Then I make the final signature piece in the new color, with small touches to tie it all together. I think I can make it work."

She led the way to the storage area. Long, tall shelves lined the wall, deep enough to hold bolts of fabric. Some she'd bought because they were a good price, others because she'd liked the pattern or color. Long before she'd ever thought to quit her job and start her own line, she'd been collecting fabric. She'd bought this building years ago because it was big enough to house her collection. A harmless hobby, she'd told herself as she bought yet another bolt of material. Yet every day she'd gone to work, something small and fragile in her heart had ached to burst into flight.

"If it's the signature piece, then you'll be wearing it. Does that help you choose a color?"

Surprised, she paused a moment. Colors swirled in her mind's eye, all shades, all hues, dizzying and overwhelming. "I never thought about what I would wear."

"You're the most important one! *You* should wear the signature piece. It's a formal event, right?"

"A gala fundraiser hosted by the City of Dallas, with a fashion show featuring a total of five designers. Each of us is donating pieces to auction off. I don't expect my pieces to bring much for the fundraiser—I'm just hoping to get some buzz about my new line." The more she thought about it, the more she couldn't believe she'd been so stupid. She'd never once thought about what she would wear, the designer, the billboard for her line. "Okay, okay, you've saved me from making a horrible mistake. I need an evening gown, definitely, and it needs to be the showstopper."

Her stomach churned and a stress headache threatened. "I don't have much time to pull this off, because now I need two new pieces, not one. I don't even have the design yet, or the fabric, and Miriam still has to hem..."

Stepping up behind her, he closed his palms on her arms, which stilled her frantic thoughts. He didn't press against her, but his closeness made the nerves hum up and down her spine. "First, color. Something unexpected, but you can still mix with the others."

"It has to be a color that I'll look decent in."

He let out a low, husky laugh against her ear that sent the southern half of her body on full alert. Oh God, now it was her turn to feel ashamed at her ravenous hunger. She was lucky her stomach didn't rumble as loudly as his had at breakfast. Starved and so damned needy, it took all her willpower not to turn around and haul his mouth down to hers.

"You'll look gorgeous in any color. Do you have a favorite color, something that's meaningful to you?"

She had to clear her throat. "No."

"Any color will go with black, white and gray. How about green to complement the red?"

Closing her eyes, she fought not to lean back and rub her entire body against him. She hadn't been held, touched, in months. *That's all this is. A night with Elias, and I'll forget this insane need.* "Too Christmassy."

"The colors you've chosen so far are hard and dramatic, a bit like you and Reyes." Jesse mused aloud. "He's harsh and grim. As a cop, everything is black and white. Right or wrong, law and order or utter chaos. I bet he despises the gray. Gray is where people begin to tell lies. All too soon, gray leads to black. There can be no middle ground, no compromise, or black wins every time. Everything has to be in its proper place, right or wrong, and he's always right."

His analysis was spot-on, but then again, Elias wasn't that hard to read. She wasn't too concerned, until Jesse began analyzing her.

"You're definitely red: passionate, uncontrolled wildfire. You clash with black all the time and you never give up without a fight."

His gentle voice didn't sound aggressive or inflammatory, but he dared a soft brush of his lips against her ear that damned near made her knees buckle.

"Maybe you need a buffer between you and him. Someone softer, gentler, who can absorb all the dramatics without falling apart, who would never try to set one against the other, and will always do exactly as you say, when you say, how you say, no questions asked. Someone who'd love getting burned by your sparks, and isn't afraid of the harder black, either. In fact, you just might like someone who can take it hard, real hard, as hard as you want."

She knew, then, that she was in serious trouble. Street-smart and worldly in ways she couldn't even comprehend, Jesse had voiced the crux of her relationship problems with Elias. In the great war of passion between them, Jesse offered himself as Switzerland.

What he didn't get at all was that Elias would go all shock-and-awe on them both if she even thought about it.

So why am I thinking about it?

She couldn't tell Jesse that he was wrong, because he wasn't, and she couldn't refuse him, because he had to know how fast her heart was pounding. She couldn't seem to catch her breath.

Ironically, now she knew exactly which color to use in her line.

Without saying a word or turning toward him, she stepped away. He let her go without trying to hold her back. Trailing her fingers along the fabrics, she walked down to the opposite end of the shelving, straining up high to reach a shimmering bolt of blue-lagoon silk.

It'd been an impulse buy, rather embarrassing, actually, because she'd never thought she'd end up using it, and it had cost her a small fortune. The color was too bright, too jewel-toned for business wear, and too seasonally restrictive for all-year wear. Or so she'd thought as she'd shoved it on the highest shelf out of her way.

Bracing herself mentally, she raised her gaze to his face as she walked toward him. His eyes, so bright, so hot and intense, were made darker and richer by the silk in her hands. Her chest constricted with an answering surge of attraction, deeper and more compelling every time she looked at him. If he'd stop looking at her like that, begging her with his eyes to devour him whole, then maybe she could pretend nothing had changed.

He was just a good guy who'd fallen on hard times.

She was just a good Samaritan.

He didn't have to get in the middle of her romantic mess.

Her cheeks burned at the thought. The image of him and Elias both touching her seared her mind, burning her to ash. She'd never once thought about such a thing, but now...

She draped the silk over the center rack and stepped back to look at her entire collection. If she made a simple turquoise shell to wear with the black pantsuit, and maybe something with gray and turquoise mixed together, it might work. However, she needed to settle on the signature piece for herself.

"What do you think?" She didn't turn to look at him, afraid that he'd see the growing need in her eyes and take the next step himself. "Is it too much?"

"Nothing's too much for you."

A lump crowded her throat, making it impossible to breathe. "Jesse—"

"Hear me out, please." He stepped closer, hovering behind and to the side without touching her. "Keep your cop. I don't care. Just keep me too."

"You know I can't do that."

"Why not?"

"You're my guest. I'm gladly helping you and I want nothing in return."

"You think I want you only because you helped me?" He dropped his forehead against her shoulder. She let out a soft

44

sigh. If he'd put his hands on her, she could have taken him to task for touching her, but his head was such a tender gesture that she couldn't be upset. "Why do you think I made you that card? Why did I carry it all these weeks, hoping beyond hope to find you again? When you get the chance, look closer at the card. See my message to you. If you'd simply thanked me for the card and sent me on my way last night, I would have gone, happy to have only seen your face, and loving you as much as I do now."

Her breath seized up in her throat. She'd dated Elias off and on for months and he'd never told her his feelings. He'd never show such vulnerability. He couldn't let down his guard long enough.

"I came to find you because I couldn't face life without seeing your smile at least every once in a while." He rubbed his mouth on her shoulder. "I'm not offering myself to pay you back. I just need to be with you, whatever that means."

She let go of the silk, afraid her sweaty palms would ruin it before she could ever implement a design. Swaying, she fought to keep her head and remain calm, untouched. "You don't know me, Jesse. Not really."

"Yes, I do." He whispered in her ear. "I know your heart. No one else has even considered helping me in five years. That's proof of what kind of woman you are, and I want to belong to you. I'm yours to take, Vicki, if you want me."

So close, so tempting, if she turned her head just a little, she could touch him. She could kiss him. She knew he wouldn't make the move himself. No, he wanted—needed—*her* to take him, as he'd said.

His hair tickled her cheek and she couldn't resist him any longer. She turned and pushed her mouth to his. Groaning deep in his throat, he opened his mouth and melted into her.

He surrendered completely, giving everything to her, no hesitation, wide open and eager. Taller and bigger, he still managed to drape himself on her, making himself vulnerable. Even though she knew he could have put her in the wall like Elias had done him last night, *she* was the one slamming Jesse backward.

His back hit the wall and he made a low, whimpering sound that wasn't pain, but a plea, as if he were saying, *Drink me down, possess me, use me, take me hard.*

And God help her, that's exactly what she did.

He spread his arms out against the wall to resist the temptation of touching her and silently begged with every muscle in his body for her to take every inch of him. Gripping his hair in both hands, she inhaled his mouth. She gnawed on his bottom lip, pressing the sore spot from his introduction to her cop last night until he groaned and arched into her, pleading for more.

Finally, her tongue sank into his mouth as deeply as he wanted to be buried in her. So ravenous, she took his mouth, her fingers twisting his hair until he couldn't help but moan out his enjoyment.

She tore her mouth from his on a soft cry of regret.

He realized, then, that she was ashamed of that desperation, as he'd felt this morning when his stomach had betrayed him so loudly.

With her eyes squeezed shut, she whispered, "I'm so sorry."

"Why? I'm begging you to kiss me again, every day, all day, just like that, please." He tucked his cheek against hers. He had to squeeze his hands into fists to resist the urge to clutch her, desperate to keep her from withdrawing. "That was the best kiss

I've ever had. I've never had a woman do me like this, like I need."

She didn't pull away, not yet, as though she couldn't bear to let him see the lust and shame on her face. "You'd rather have a man?"

"Hell, no. I'm not gay; I'm not even bi. But a lot of men like my looks. I did what I needed to survive." He was proud that his voice didn't quiver. Hopefully she had no idea how much he'd hated selling himself. The degradation, the shame of servicing a man, often against his will, to keep from getting the shit beat of him or worse. He didn't want that part of his life to touch her, not if he could help it. "I like my partner to be in control, but I want a woman to take me. I want *you*."

She groaned against his ear, turned on, he hoped, but she shuddered, a slight withdrawal that had him leaning into her, trying to entice her with his body to stay.

Desperately, he whispered his fantasies into her ear. "I like sex rough, hard, sweaty, up against a wall, frantic, wherever you'll take me. I love you in control, taking what you want, demanding I give it up, everything, for you."

"I can't take advantage of you like this. It's wrong. You trusted me—"

He couldn't help but laugh and shift his hips forward, pressing his erection into her stomach. "How could something that feels this good be wrong?"

She slid her right hand down his back and wrapped her fingers around the waistband of his pants, hauling him tighter against her. "I'm going to hell for this."

"Then you might as well enjoy me fully."

Laughing raggedly, she buried her face against his neck. "Hold me, Jesse. Just hold me. It's been so long."

Wrapping his arms around her as tightly as she held him, he didn't ask any questions. The last thing he wanted was for her to feel like he was pushing her to choose him over her cop. But if that son of a bitch had been neglecting her, then Jesse would be more than happy to fulfill her every need.

"I'm going to go upstairs and make some calls, so feel free to help yourself to the laundry, take a nap, whatever you'd like. First thing tomorrow, I want you to see a doctor. Then we'll go shopping so your baggy pants don't make me think about how easily they'd fall down, and we'll go by VCONN and you can meet my brother. Right now, I need...to think. About all this."

She must be seriously considering taking him to her bed if she wanted him to get checked out, but at the same time, she wanted space. She needed to slow down. He understood that. He wasn't her whole world, not like she was for him. "I'll do whatever you want, Vicki. I'll stay down here until you call me."

"I..." Pulling back, she blew out her breath. "You don't have to stay down here or wait for me to call you. I want this to be your home."

"It is, as long as you're here."

Chapter Four

Sitting on the edge of her bed with the door shut, Vicki stared down at Jesse's birthday card. Her hand trembled, making the butterfly wings blur, but she already knew his subtle message to her. At first glance, the black lines had merely seemed to be outlines to emphasize the soft watercolors. But the longer she'd stared at the card, she realized the lines were actually curves—no, letters—long, graceful cursive to spell out his message over and over.

I love you.

Her phone rang, making her jump. Elias. Sick at heart, she hit the button. "Please don't tell me that you can't make it tonight."

"What's wrong, Vik? Is your houseguest starting to scare you?" He laughed, telling her he wasn't really serious.

"You were right, Elias," she whispered, fighting back the tears. "You were right, and I'm in trouble."

"Trouble like you need me to come over and bust his mouth open again?" His hard cop voice echoed over the line. "I can be there in twenty minutes. If you're in danger, then I'll send the closest squad car to pick him up."

"No, no, I'm not in danger. *He* is. I'm scaring myself."

"Hold on a minute, Vik. Let me find a private room."

She heard the chatter of the office and finally the door shut, sealing off all noises.

"Okay, spill. What has you so freaked out?"

"He does love me. He told me. Even the birthday card—that he made months ago—says that he loves me."

"Yeah," Elias said slowly, drawing the word out. "How'd you react to that earth-shattering news?"

She squeezed her eyes shut and held the phone away from her ear in case he started yelling at her. "I kissed him."

It took her a minute to realize the muffled sounds coming from his phone weren't curses, but might actually be laughter.

"You aren't laughing at me, are you? I kissed him. No, I slammed him up against the wall like you did last night, only instead of splitting his lip open, I damned near bit it off."

Elias laughed harder. "Did he thank you for it?"

"Yeah, yeah he did. In fact, he begged me to do it again. Why aren't you pissed?"

"Oh, Vik, I don't know. It's not like I have any right to be pissed at you for kissing another man when I haven't been around in months. Besides, you're too upset for me to be mad, and he's not a bad kid. No, he's a real good-looking kid, a nice tender morsel." He laughed harder, like one of his buddies had told him the most hilarious joke he'd ever heard. "Making love to you has always been like wrestling a hungry crocodile. Did you shock the hell out of him?"

Stricken, she could barely breathe through the tightness in her chest. "I'm that bad?"

"Aw hell, no, Vicki, you're that *good.*" His voice was as tender as she'd ever heard him. "You're the hottest, sexiest, most passionate woman I've ever had the pleasure to meet. But you're not a soft, passive woman in bed, far from it. Half the fun is wrestling you for dominance, and the other half is making sure you enjoy the consolation prize, as much as I am. Any smarter man would never have left you simmering all these months. It's as much my fault as yours that you're so attracted to Jesse."

"So you'll come over tonight? Please?"

He let out a wicked, low laugh that made her blood smolder. "Oh, I don't know, Vik. Your couch isn't that comfortable. Besides, you've got that hot cabana boy to tend to you now. Why do you need me?"

"I won't make you sleep on the couch tonight. I swear."

"We're going to be loud, babe," he purred, drawing a rough groan from her. "I'm going to make you scream. We're going to hit every surface of your bedroom, hell, your whole apartment, and your boy's going to hear every whimper, thud, curse and shout of release. Are you sure you're up for that?"

Her nipples were so hard the lace of her bra felt like sandpaper. "Can you come home now?"

Now it was his turn to groan. "I wish I could, but I've got a meeting with the lieutenant in five minutes. I expect we'll go out on a tip this afternoon, so don't hold dinner for me."

"Elias, please, you *have* to come tonight."

"I will," he promised. "It might be late, but as soon as we're done with the bust, I'll drive straight to you." He hesitated, an edge coming to his voice. "You know he's probably loaded with STDs or worse. God only knows what he's been exposed to in prison, let alone the streets."

"I know," she whispered, lying back on her bed. "I'm taking him to the clinic tomorrow. I already made an appointment."

"You're serious, then. Jesus, Vik."

"I know." She closed her eyes and rubbed her temple with her free hand. "What does this mean for us?"

"Hell if I know. I'd say I should simply take the hint and get the hell out of Dodge, but you're begging me to come over tonight."

"I've missed you." Her voice broke but she refused to bitch and moan about the past. Elias had chosen to bail on her. He'd played both judge and jury and blamed her for everything that had gone wrong, but she couldn't stop loving him. *Even when he's an uncompromising ass.* "I don't want to lose you all over again."

"But you want him too."

Her relationship with Elias had always had a lot of failings, but one thing she'd never done was lie to him. "Yeah, I do."

"Well, fuck."

"Yeah, I want that too."

Laughter exploded out of him, startling them both. "Don't do anything rash, Vik. I don't want you to get burned."

"You either. He's not a threat to you, so don't let your macho ego get in the way of this."

"*This?*" He drawled out, making her toes curl. "What exactly are you offering me, Vik? Sharing you with that young pup? I'm a junkyard Rottie named Spike and I guarantee my bite is just as mean as my bark. I don't tolerate cream-puff poodles around my woman."

"You know you're my top dog. Jesse...well...I guess I'm *his* top dog." At least Elias hadn't cursed her out or driven over to break Jesse's arm as he'd threatened last night. Definitely an improvement. "You don't bite, do you, Spike?"

He snorted. "You know I do, babe."

"Yeah, me too." Her neck throbbed right below her ear, his favorite place to grip her with his teeth while they made love. Her voice had gone sultry and thick, but she didn't care. "Just to be clear, *babe*, you don't have to worry about my cream-puff poodle biting you. That'll be all me with my crocodile teeth."

Watching Jesse come up the stairs toward her apartment, Vicki tried to swallow around her heart that felt like it'd lodged in her throat. His freshly washed jeans were comfortably worn, threadbare and ragged in spots, which was all the rage anyway. He'd pulled his hair back in a ponytail, tight in contrast to the simple cotton T-shirt and jeans.

He'd left his shoes and socks off too. Barefoot and vulnerable, he made her heart ache. He trusted her to take care of and protect him. In the cold on the streets, he'd never walk around without his shoes for fear someone worse off might take them.

To break the intensity, she asked, "Hungry?"

He stared at her mouth, pausing several steps below so his head remained lower than hers. "Starving."

Blood pounded a vicious tempo in her ears. Slowly, she reached out to lightly brush her fingers across his jaw to the ponytail holder. "May I?"

"You can do anything you want to me."

She worked the rubber band loose, trying not to pull his hair, but his eyes darkened like a mysterious lagoon. Experimentally, she wrapped her hand in his hair and tugged, mesmerized by the way his mouth softened, opened. His tongue darted out, his eyes falling shut. "What do you like?"

"Anything you want."

"I'm serious."

"So am I. I'm up for anything you tell me to do. You said your brother was a sadist, so if pain runs in the blood, try me. I can take a lot of punishment."

She blew out her breath, frustrated and scared spitless. *Maybe I should have gone with Victor a few times so I'd know what the hell I'm getting into.* "I don't want to punish you. I want you to feel safe and secure with me. I'm not going to let anyone hurt you."

"Not even your cop?"

He didn't say it like an accusation, but dread still made her stomach queasy. She owed Elias her allegiance first and foremost. He was a good man, an excellent cop and a fabulous lover. But when it came to his pride, he could be a loose cannon. *In the end, aren't I cheating on him with another man? How can I ask him to allow this?*

"Because if you want him to fuck me, I'll accept him gladly."

Blood drained from her face. She cupped his cheeks in both hands and leaned down with her sternest look. "I will never ask you to do such a thing. If you don't want to do something, I need to know. You told me earlier you don't like men, so don't make that kind of offer to me. It's not necessary. In fact, it's repulsive to me, and to Elias, that you'd think we'd require such services from you in order for you to stay. You have to tell me the truth or I can't protect you."

His eyes shimmered and his mouth trembled. "I'll do anything, Vicki. Please don't send me away."

"I'm not going to send you away, but we have to take this slowly. I don't know what the hell I'm doing. I don't want to lose Elias just to have you, but the thought of losing you..." Letting out a rough growl, she pulled Jesse into her arms. Eagerly, he went to his knees, pressing as close to her as possible. "I'm going to get help for you, for me, whatever it takes. You've been abused, and I don't want to screw this up out of ignorance."

He hugged with his entire body, arms locked around her hips. "I've never had a choice. I don't know what I like, not really, but when you touch me, even a hug, it's like angels start singing and my bones melt and my blood boils in my veins. It's you. Whatever you want. I trust you not to hurt me."

Hands trembling, she held him, smoothing her hands over his back and shoulders. *Such responsibility. God help me.* She couldn't stop touching him, though, like she couldn't watch him walk away into the snow and cold. She wanted to make him feel safe and loved like he'd never been before.

"Just having you touch me..." Muffled against her stomach, his words burrowed into her. "I'm starved for affection and physical contact as much as anything else."

"Let's go eat dinner." Soothingly, she ran her fingers through his hair. "Then if you can stand to watch cheesy horror movies, we'll cuddle on the couch for awhile."

Reluctantly, he released her and stood. "If you'll let me hold your hand, I'll even watch ballet."

She offered her hand, and he clasped her fingers between his palms, bending down to kiss her knuckles. His caressed her with his lips, making what should have been a polite gesture into something so erotic it could have been X-rated.

And then he got his tongue involved.

He nudged her knuckle firmly, lips closing around the small bump to suck and work, silently demonstrating what he'd eagerly do between her thighs if she gave him the chance. His teeth grazed her skin, making her groan out loud and pull her hand away, although she kept his fingers gripped in hers.

"Give me any part of your body," he said, voice breathless, "and I'll worship it with only my lips, tongue and teeth."

Unsteady, she had to brace herself against the door frame before trusting her balance. "Good Lord, Jesse, will you stop tempting me like this?"

He shook his head, tumbling his hair down to veil his stunning eyes. "You asked me what I'd enjoy. I'm just being honest. I'd love to have you spread out naked with the order that I'm only to touch you with my mouth."

Now that she'd fueled his confidence where he felt safe enough to flirt and entice, this dangerous attraction was only getting worse by the moment. Floundering between consuming need and embarrassment—at how easily and fiercely he'd managed to turn her on—she forced herself to turn away and shut the door. She even tried squeezing her eyes shut so she couldn't see the tempting invitation blazing in his.

But that didn't stop him. "I think I could come just from sucking on your finger. I know I would if you kissed me right now."

"We are so not going there. We can't. I want to give you time—"

"I've had time on the streets. I've done time in prison. I don't need time to know that I love you."

"*I* need time. I can't say that I want to protect you, and then take advantage of you." In desperation, she added, "Elias is spending the night, and this time, he won't be on the couch."

Jesse's eyes only darkened more and he edged closer. "Can I watch?"

"No!" She shuddered at the thought. Elias would probably bust a vein in his forehead if she'd even thought to ask him. "Absolutely not."

Groaning, Jesse dropped his head to her shoulder. "Please, Vicki, I'm dying. Give me something. Anything. Can I at least come when you do?"

She opened her mouth to retort that he could come whenever the hell he wanted, but she couldn't say it. She stood there, mouth open, eyes wide, dumbstruck by the surge of pure power and primal lust that crashed through her. She liked the idea of controlling his release. Making him wait. Giving him a word, a simple caress, and watching his mouth fall open, his eyes blaze, while he pumped at her command.

"Oh," he breathed out in a soft whisper, raising his head to search her face, his eyes as wide as hers. "You like that idea. While he's inside you, think of me downstairs, tangled in the sheets, sweating and rock-hard while I listen, begging to hear your cry of release. No matter how much I hurt, I won't touch myself. All it'll take is your voice, your scream, and I'll explode. Yes? Please?"

She swallowed hard and tried to slow down her breathing before she hyperventilated. "On one condition."

"Anything."

"You back down on the flirting until I get my head wrapped around this. Okay?"

"Wrapped around you and me?"

"And me and Elias."

"Yes'm." Jesse smiled and tipped his head in a nod. "Is he a good lover?"

She remembered Elias's threat-promise: *We're going to be loud, babe.* "Oh, yeah. It might get rather...rowdy."

"Good." Jesse's eyes burned sultry. "I can't wait for him to arrive."

Elias quietly slipped his seldom-used key into her locked door and eased it open. It made him feel sneaky and mean, hoping to catch her in a compromising position, and also sick to his stomach at the thought. He didn't know if he could really face that reality. He could talk about it, even joke about it, but if he saw her having sex with another man, it might be the last breath that bastard would ever take.

Even if that man was Jesse, who managed to give off that helpless victim vibe that must have drawn the vilest perps in Dallas.

Elias had no right to claim her sole affections, not after abandoning her these past months. Frustrated rage at his job had simmered over into his personal life. When Donnie had been killed, Elias could only picture himself lying dead in the street. He'd like to think that maybe he'd wanted to protect her from ever ending up a sobbing widow leaning over his coffin, but he couldn't lie to himself.

Her client had blown *his* partner away.

She'd only being doing her job, which merely happened to run counter to his. *But she didn't have to do it so fucking well.*

So he'd taken his rage out on her, even though he knew it was stupid. He'd been a prick. She was a strong woman and she could carry a hell of a lot, but that didn't make it right for him to dump the blame on her shoulders. *Especially when I carry Donnie's death on my back too.*

It would serve him right if she'd moved on and found another man. A man who didn't work himself to death in case a drug dealer didn't get to him first. *Or a kid who worships the ground she walks on because she saved him.*

The lights were off but the television was playing one of those ridiculous black-and-white zombie movies she loved so much. Two heads were visible above the couch, although Jesse's was low and tucked into her neck more than Elias cared to see. Nothing suspicious was going on—they were only watching a movie.

Doubt ate away at him. She'd been so upset, so desperate earlier when they'd talked on the phone. Maybe they'd already done the deed hours ago. Instead of serving dinner, maybe she'd taken Jesse on top of the table.

Elias knew full well that she was a passionate woman. The kid was so eager and desperate to belong to her, that God only knew how far he'd pushed her. Elias couldn't even bring himself to blame him. He'd do a hell of a lot to keep her himself, even if the last few months hadn't proven how much he cared about her.

He shut the door quietly, but her head whipped around. Her eyes met his, and he knew, beyond a shadow of a doubt, that she hadn't found release in anyone else's arms. Not by the fire in her eyes. He swore the temperature in the room spiked twenty degrees.

Beside her, Jesse uncurled, stretching like a sleepy cat.

Elias forced himself to move slowly instead of falling on her like a starving wolf. Methodically, he stashed his gun and badge in the bolted-down safe he'd installed in her coat closet once they got serious. Shutting the door, he turned and raked his eyes over her as she stood. She wore jeans and a soft sweater instead of a slinky gown or low-cut blouse, but it was all he could do not to bury his hands in that cotton and rip his way into her lush body.

She stalked toward him, her eyes glittering, her body simmering that siren call of need. Need for him. Eyes only for him. Despite the handsome younger man hovering warily at her back.

Trying not to be an asshole, at least this time, he said in a gruff voice, "Get your butt downstairs, Jesse."

The kid shot toward the door like zombies had started crawling out of the TV.

Not a moment too soon, because she slammed into Elias and attacked his shirt. He'd left his tie and jacket in the truck, but he couldn't remember if he had any spare clothes here. Jerking at the button on her jeans, he bit her bottom lip so hard her breath hissed out, spurring her to yank harder.

"Watch the shirt, babe. I have to show up for work tomorrow without looking like I was mugged."

A button pinged on the wall. "I'll make you a new one."

He jammed his hand down the front of her jeans, wincing at the zipper digging into his skin, but he couldn't slow down. He had to stroke her, see how turned on she was, how quickly she came at his touch. It'd tell him a lot about how much she'd missed him.

She rolled her hips, squirming against him, helping work his fingers deeper, past the satin, hooking his finger beneath...

"Yes," he growled out against her ear. "You're so wet and hot you're going to come...now," he finished, a bit surprised. He hadn't meant it as a command, but she shuddered, groaning deep in her throat.

Her cry of pleasure rose in intensity, her hunger flaming higher. Tightening her arms around his neck, she hopped up against him, forcing him to catch her with his free arm while she wrapped her legs around his waist.

"Hurry." She moaned, but then she stiffened in his arms a moment, and he wondered if she was going to come again so quickly. He buried a finger inside her and she shuddered, her voice rising, wild and desperate. "Elias, please!"

He started for her bedroom, but a soft noise made him hesitate. It sounded like a low moan. He whipped his head around as the door snicked shut. Damn that punk. If he'd thought to watch the show...

"I need you now," she whispered, thrusting and stroking her tongue in his ear, her breath hot and frantic, and Elias forgot to care.

Leaning against the wall with his eyes closed, Jesse struggled to calm his breathing. She'd looked at him over the cop's shoulder. She'd seen him standing there, jeans gaping open to ease the misery, cock out and hard and jerking in climax. If the cop had turned around and seen him indecently exposed, he'd probably be a gelding.

His legs trembled, so he didn't try to maneuver down the stairs yet. He'd kept his promise to her, no hands other than to catch as much of the load as possible, although he'd still have to sneak back up here to clean the landing.

A muffled thump, a low, hard voice, and his groin stirred all over again. He stumbled down the stairs, washed his hands, and cleaned up the mess as quickly as possible. Then he stripped naked, stretched out on the bed she'd given him, and stared up at the ceiling.

The thumps were louder. Yes, he'd been right. Her bedroom was directly above. He closed his eyes and imagined how the cop was making love to her. Not the bed, not yet. They'd been too urgent to make it that far.

Jesse scrambled to his knees and planted his hands on the wall above the headboard. Yes, against the wall, vibrating with their passion. Braced on his knees, he imagined her pressed against his back, stroking his chest and stomach, lingering, playing low on his belly while she laughed huskily in his ear.

When she screamed, he would be the one rocking the bed.

Chapter Five

Elias set her down long enough for him to shuck his pants, while she shed her clothes in record time. She burned, worse than she'd ever ached for him. Yet Jesse's image hovered in the background of her mind, stirring her lust to heights she'd never even thought about before. So hot, to see him standing there, climaxing in secret behind Elias's back. Only because *she* was climaxing, which had made her come harder, a weird synchronicity that lit her nerves on fire.

Oh, the power. What a rush.

Yet her stomach twisted with anxiety, because if Elias had turned around a moment too soon, what would he have done? Would he have broken Jesse's arm as he'd threatened that first night? Or worse?

Elias slammed her up against the wall so hard the whole house shook. By the quirk of his mouth and the wicked glint in his eyes, he knew damned well how that must have sounded to the younger man downstairs. He wasn't pissed because he was the top dog. They all knew it. Only he would be in her bed tonight.

Dare I hope for something even better than jealous violence if he'd seen what was happening behind him?

"Condom?"

Breathless, she narrowed her eyes, tempted to tell him yes just to piss him off. She was on the pill, but they'd been broken up for more months than she cared to count. "Have you been with anyone else?"

"No." Somehow, he managed to sound insulted. "I'm not the one with the hot cabana boy downstairs listening to our every groan."

"I'm not the one who walked out on us, and no, if you're curious, I haven't been with anyone else either."

She pushed the shirt the rest of the way off his shoulders, reveling in the sheer strength in his body. He wasn't a big man, but he carried a wallop of power in his lean, six-foot-tall frame. He'd trained for years, more than capable of running down a druggie or taking out a burglar with his bare hands. He knew exactly how to use every muscle. His neck and shoulders corded and flexed, effortlessly shifting her higher on the wall.

"No condom," she whispered, winding her fingers in the short, dark hair at the base of his neck. "Just you, Spike."

Half in play but also deadly serious, he snarled and snapped his teeth at her ear. He gripped her shoulder in his jaws, biting this side of pain, and she couldn't suppress the delicious shiver that rocked her body against his. With a brutal thrust, he shoved inside her so hard that a cry tore out of her throat.

He knew exactly what she liked, how much she could take. He certainly knew how slick and wet she was for him. The only problem—it'd been too long for him too. After a few thrusts, he shuddered and poured into her.

Panic made her pulse flutter like a butterfly trapped in a glass. Need pounded inside her as strong as his thrusts, demanding, hammering for attention. Her skin was raw and tender like she'd rolled around in broken glass. Swollen and so damned tight, she wanted to scream at him for finishing so quickly.

"Damn you." She clawed his back hard enough he grunted and thudded inside her on another pulse. "God, I need you so bad. What am I supposed to do now?"

He actually had the audacity to *laugh.* "You're insatiable, Vik."

Furious, desperate emotion tore through her like a hurricane. He'd said she was like a hungry crocodile. Maybe he was tired of trying to keep her satisfied. Maybe that's why she suddenly found herself attracted to two men. Need and shame twisted inside her, ugly and painful. She shoved at his chest and threw her elbow at his throat. The more he tried to contain her struggles, the harder she fought him.

In a smooth move they must teach at the police academy, he flipped her over and used his weight to pin her against the wall. Awkwardly, she flailed back at him with both arms, but he snagged first one wrist and then the other in the small of her back. The more she squirmed, the higher he pushed her arms until her muscles quivered and her shoulders burned with pain.

"I've got you, babe," he whispered in a devilishly relaxed—fully satiated—voice. "You know I'll take good, long, hard care of you."

Panting, she pushed out her hips and arched her back, grinding herself against him, but he'd chosen this position deliberately. He had full access to her body, but she couldn't bring herself much pleasure against him. "Seems like your *long, hard care* is over already."

"You know long and hard will be back soon enough." He scattered feather-light caresses on her ear, cheek, neck, and shoulder, a torment. "I had your boy slammed up against the wall like this last night. When you kissed him, did you trap him like this? Did you hold him down?"

"No, I kissed him, that's all."

"That's all." He shifted his grip on her wrists to his left hand, freeing his right. "Then you didn't take as good care of him as I'm going to give to you."

Dread and anticipation coiled in her stomach. She was primed and loaded for bear, more than ready to detonate. A ticking bomb throbbed and hummed inside her. In this mood, he might torment her a long, long time before he gave her what she wanted.

Lightly, he traced his fingertips over her right breast, tickling her skin, driving her insane. Growling beneath her breath, she twisted in his grip. "I'm trying to take good care of him." *Which is exactly why I haven't taken him yet.*

Elias breathed a low rumbling growl into her ear. "You'd better be taking good care of *me*, babe. I don't give a rat's ass about Jesse."

But I do. Guilt and fury swamped her, stirring her fighting instincts. She kicked backward and caught his shin hard enough he cursed. "I think I saw to you already."

"Nah, that was just the appetizer." He swiped his tongue along the curve of her ear. "We're going to take a long, sweaty ride while you buck for all you're worth. You *want* to fight me. You want me to conquer you, tame you to my hands and my body like a green-broke mare. Every time we fuck each other into a stupor, you make me prove I'm man enough for you. So buck. Fight. Or better yet..."

He leaned in, shoving with his body hard enough that her breath rushed out on a groan, but he released her hands. "Try to drag me into a death roll at the bottom of the river."

His fingers locked on her nipple in a fierce pinch that sent shockwaves tearing through her. Where he'd teased before, he punished now. Every alarm and button in her body went on high alert. He'd deliberately let go of her hands—so she could struggle more, harder, and work him to a fevered pitch. She jammed her elbows back into his ribs, kicked him, threw her head back at his face, even raked her nails down his forearm braced beside her.

He didn't duck or try to stop her blows, but he kept her tight to the wall. It took all her strength, throwing her body like a weapon and using the wall for leverage, to gain an inch against him, while his fingers rolled and tugged her breast. His teeth sank into her shoulder, working closer and closer to her nape.

His hardened cock pressed against her buttocks, and she redoubled her efforts. *To get him inside me.*

Their panting echoed in the room, the dull thuds of flesh on flesh echoing, promising more, so much more. She could only imagine what it sounded like to Jesse downstairs.

As if Elias knew she'd thought of the other man, he growled in her ear. "Can he take you like this, Vik? Can he make you groan and sweat facedown against the wall? Can he ride you at your worst, no matter how bad you buck and kick?"

"No," she wheezed out, her cheek smashed so hard against the wall it was hard to talk. "But I bet he'll give *me* a good ride."

Elias let out a vicious growl against her ear, jerked her hips back, and surged inside her.

Damn her and those torturous images she'd managed to lodge in his mind. All too easily, he could see her working the kid over as hard as he was taking her now. In fact, if she had him flat against the wall beneath her, Elias could be taking them both without even laying a finger on the man.

He shuddered.

The thought should have disgusted him. He'd never once considered having another man anywhere near him while he made love to a woman. *But for Vicki...*

"Don't you dare," she retorted, shoving harder against him. "I'm not done with you yet."

Weaving his fingers with hers, he held her hands against the wall and eased his attack. She arched and rubbed against him like a cat, purring against his cheek. Vicki hot and wild, or smoldering tenderness, God, he'd missed her. "What are you doing to me, babe?"

She choked out a laugh. "You really don't know?"

He tried to find the words. How sorry he was that he'd run out on her when things got too complicated. How much he valued her strength, intelligence, and dedication to her job. How sorry he was that Donnie had died, and how terrified he'd been at the thought of leaving her like that.

It could happen any moment. The cartels were stronger than ever. More drugs hit the streets every single day, no matter how hard his team worked. They'd never keep the streets clean.

"Vicki..."

"I know," she whispered, twisting her mouth back toward his. "I still love you, Elias."

She kissed him, not giving him time to answer. Because she didn't want him to feel obligated to voice emotions she knew he hated to admit.

She knows me all too well.

To make up for being such a heartless asshole, he gave her exactly what she wanted. Long, powerful thrusts, his breath ragged in her ear, his body punishing, loving, tormenting, until she writhed against him.

"Please, Elias. Please!"

He buried his fingers between her thighs, kept her breast tight in his other hand, and gripped the back of her neck in his teeth like a mama cat carrying her babies while he thrust harder, veins pumping, muscles straining to bursting.

She let out a wordless, hoarse scream that rattled the windows. Deliberately, he made his own groan rough and deep, a primal growl of the alpha taking his mate for the young pup downstairs. Sagging against her, he concentrated on catching his breath. His pulse thundered in his skull and his thighs ached like he'd run a marathon.

He was totally unprepared for her to slither around, hook her heel behind his knee, and sling him around so he was on his back against the wall.

Letting out a laughing groan, he dropped his head back against the wall and tried not to wheeze.

"That's better," she purred against his throat.

She nuzzled and rubbed her face on his chest, while she ran her hands over his shoulders and arms. No hesitant, gentle touches, not from his Vicki. She had the powerful hands of a masseuse. Even if she hadn't made him blow his mind twice in the span of less than an hour, she could turn him into a puddle with those incredible hands. God help him when she decided to involve that luscious mouth of hers.

"Don't you want to hit your bed at least once, babe?"

"Sure." She bit his nipple, making him clench his hands into fists at his sides. "But it's so rare for me to have you like this."

He narrowed his gaze, searching her face. "Like what?"

"Passive. Calm. Worn out." She smiled against his chest and slid her hands down his flanks and around to his buttocks. She gripped his ass firmly, tilting his hips closer to hers. "Mine to take."

His stomach tightened uneasily. That must be why she found Jesse so appealing. She could take him anytime she wanted, instead of wrestling and challenging him into exhaustion first. "Is that what you want, really? Because I can lie back and take one for the team, anytime, anywhere, Vik. If you want to take me, I'm yours."

Eyes dark and mysterious, she cocked her head and simply looked at him, her mouth quirked in a smug little half smile that miraculously made his cock stir all over again.

"Do you want a shower now or later?"

"I definitely need a shower before I stink up your bed."

Laughing with a sultry timbre to her voice, she released him and headed for the bathroom. "I hope I don't drown you."

Chapter Six

Groggy and deliciously sore in places she hadn't been in months, Vicki stirred when the bed dipped. She'd vaguely heard the shower running, but hadn't managed to do much more than pull a pillow over her head. Bleary-eyed, she rolled over on her back and cracked open an eye.

"Morning, Vik."

Elias's husky voice in the early morning made her want to arch her back and purr an invitation. But she knew all too well that he had to get to work. "What time is it?"

"Six thirty." He leaned down and kissed her. "Thanks for last night."

"Thank *you*." She wrapped her arms around his neck. His hair was still damp at his nape, and he smelled so clean and fresh she could only think about making him sweaty all over again. "I see you found your stash of clothes. Are you coming back tonight?" *Every night?*

His fingers cupped her nape, kneading gently. "Do you want me to?"

Cases of argument flashed through her mind. Would it be better to pretend disinterest, so she didn't appear too desperate? Would the truth only drive him away? She'd told him she still loved him last night. So why would he ask if she wanted him to come back?

Some of her anxiety must have transmitted through the tightness of her arms, because he drew her against his chest and buried his face in her neck. "If you're offering another home run like last night, then my answer is hell yeah."

Relaxing, she laughed and nibbled on his ear. "You mean you're willing to take another blowjob in the shower?"

"For the team," he replied solemnly.

She pulled back so he could see her face and the truth reflected in her eyes. "I want you every night, Detective Reyes."

"Then I'd best restock my supply of shirts." He gave her another kiss and then stood to slip on his suit jacket. "By the way, Jesse met me at the stairs as soon as I stuck my head out and begged me to let him come in and cook breakfast for you."

That explained Elias's sudden doubt attack and the clatter she heard.

"He also asked me to give you this. Call me if you have any issues today."

She mumbled a reply and managed a smile at his back, but the watercolor artwork held her attention. Jesse had painted on heavy stock paper again, but it wasn't folded like a card. There wasn't a message on the back. No, the message was part of the design, like the birthday card he'd made.

This time he'd painted sunflowers, bright and golden summer with a gorgeous azure sky and bluebonnets sprinkled along the bottom edge. In that heavy, graceful outline of curls and hidden words, he'd written: *I came three times for you.*

Elias stuck his head back in the door. "Rise and shine, babe, or Jesse's going to deliver your breakfast in bed."

She slung off the blankets and shot toward the bathroom, chased by Elias's laughter.

Vicki parked her red Mini in the department store lot and turned to Jesse. He didn't meet her gaze and his shoulders were tight and hunched, reminding her of the first night she'd seen him. "Ready?"

"Sure." But he didn't look up. Every muscle in his thin, wiry body screamed reluctance. The man had given at least a gallon of blood at the clinic and endured God only knew how many invasive exams, but paled at the prospect of shopping.

"You're not going to give me trouble, are you?" She kept her voice light, trying to tease him out of his mood. "I've bought or made Elias a dozen shirts and he refuses to wear them all."

Speaking of her lover brought Jesse's head up. "I'll gladly wear whatever you give me. I just..." His hands trembled in his lap, so she reached over and laced her fingers with his. "I'm so grateful, Vicki. I'll pay you back. Every dime."

"Look at me, Jesse." The shimmer in his turquoise eyes twisted her heart into knots. Gently, she cupped his cheek in her palm. "I want to help you, no strings attached. I love to shop and you're gorgeous. It's going to be fun, and I never want you to pay back a single dime."

He opened his mouth to protest, so she arched a brow at him and chose her words deliberately. "Would you deny me the pleasure of picking out a few outfits for you?"

As she intended, his eyes sparked. "I'll give you any pleasure you want."

She leaned in and whispered the words against his lips. "Then let me take you shopping."

His breath fluttered fast and frantic, his soft lips soft falling open in invitation. "Take me anywhere. Even shopping."

So far, he hadn't pushed the flirting or temptation, even after the wild night she'd had with Elias. Curious how far he'd keep to the "no flirting" agreement, she didn't kiss him. Pulling back, she dropped the keys and her cellphone in her purse. As she shut the car door, she glanced at Jesse and smiled at the decidedly pouted bottom lip. Which only made her think about sucking that lip into her mouth and gripping it in her teeth.

Now who needs to remember the no flirting rule?

In less than an hour, she had him trapped in the dressing room while she tossed outfits over the door for him to try on. Since he was still underweight, she tried to give him room to fill back out without endangering his modesty and her sanity. She started with casual clothes and moved toward business casual. Until she knew what kind of job he got, a few basics would be enough.

She watched him twist and turn before the mirror. Even in basic chinos and a plain white dress shirt, he looked stunning. She ran her hands over his shoulders and chest, smoothing the fabric and checking the fit. "You really could be a model, you know."

"Never thought about it, I guess." Jesse tried to catch her gaze in the mirror, but she determinedly concentrated on his clothes and not him. "I'm too old now."

She made a disgusted mock growl. "Don't talk about old when you're still under thirty. You really need a custom-fitted shirt to emphasize your trim waist."

He shrugged. "This is fine. Looks good to me."

She stepped back and studied him, tilting her head. An idea was starting to form in her mind, that old familiar itch promising a burst of creative energy. She could see him in a fancy shirt made out of the turquoise silk. Not a normal dress shirt—no, that would be too conservative. Something that suited his masculine yet delicate features. Maybe a gentleman's shirt from the eighteenth or nineteenth centuries. Or an artist's, something with a bit of lace or ruffle at the sleeve. Not too feminine, but long enough to hang out of his coat sleeves.

A gray cashmere suit with an antique, custom shirt to match his eyes beneath. *Yes.*

"How would you feel about participating in the show with me next month? Honestly. I totally understand if that's not something you'd feel comfortable with. If I asked Elias, he'd probably arrest me."

Jesse's eyes lit up even more than usual. "Really? I'd love to! The thought of wearing something you made with your own hands..." He let out a delicious little groan that made her nipples peak and sent a pulse of liquid heat through her groin. "Definitely, yes."

"I have an idea." She had to clear her throat but her voice still sounded husky. "When we get back home tonight, I'll sketch it out, see what you think."

To make him feel better about how much she was going to spend, she headed to the women's department. Unfortunately, nothing really caught her fancy. *That's the downside of trying to launch my own line—nothing but my own designs will do.*

She turned around, looking for Jesse, and found him mesmerized by a white fluffy negligee a few rows back in the lingerie department. She walked back toward him, trying to figure out why he found the silly thing so interesting. It was innocent and frilly, totally not her style. He'd already said she was red, passion and fire. Not meek and insipid white, let alone such a feminine, helpless looking outfit.

Her hackles rose looking at the damned thing, but she tried to keep the bite out of her voice. "You're not picturing me in that, are you?"

His cheeks flushed but he met her gaze with a sheepish shrug of his shoulders. "So sue me, I'm a guy. You'd be hot in it."

"In this?" Incredulity rang in her voice and he smiled wider. "You've got to be kidding me."

"Remember the surprise factor."

That took her aback. When choosing colors and patterns only by her personal preference, she'd created a solid but boringly conservative line, which was far from what she'd hoped to accomplish.

"I already knew you were strong, kind, gorgeous, and that once you make up your mind to do something, you do it one hundred percent all the way." His dropped his voice to a rough whisper. "I heard enough last night to know that you're also uninhibited and sexy as hell."

Now it was her turn to blush. He'd finally gotten in a dig about what all he'd heard last night. "What's your point?"

"If you were to deliberately pick out something to wear for Reyes, I bet you'd choose red or black, right? This is totally unexpected. It screams innocence and shyness, a direct contradiction to your personality. If you were to slip this little baby on for your cop, I guarantee he'll swallow his tongue in surprise, and then blow a gasket trying to get you out of it."

Doubtfully, she took the hanger off the rack to examine the negligee closer. She tried to picture herself in it and failed. Just thinking about it made her feel awkward, shy and stupid, none of which she typically felt, especially around Elias. He brought out the vixen—rather, the crocodile—in her. Not the blushing virgin.

Maybe that's exactly Jesse's point.

He stepped close enough to whisper. "Hold it up to you. Let me imagine you wearing it." *For me.*

75

He didn't say the last words out loud, but she heard the longing in his voice and read the intensity in his body. Could he be right? Would Elias like her in such a feminine, innocent-looking nightgown?

She held the negligee beneath her chin and watched Jesse's eyes flare wider, darken to the mysterious lost-lagoon depths.

"If you think it's too..."

"Virginal," she said wryly.

His mouth quirked and he dipped his head. "Then wear something brazen beneath, like a see-through thong. Or better yet, nothing at all."

She arched a brow at him in warning but he only grinned wider. "That reminds me. You need underwear and socks. Hmmm, I wonder what size you are?"

Since he was so close, it was easy enough to reach around his waist and slide her fingers down the back of his saggy jeans in search of the waistband tag.

Mistake. Huge. Because instead of cotton, her fingers met only bare skin.

"Jesse. You're not wearing any underwear."

A muffled gasp drew her attention. A blushing, wide-eyed saleslady stared at them.

"No, ma'am." Whispering, he dropped his head and allowed his shoulders to droop, that automatic, innate signal of surrender she recognized despite her refusals to ever consider learning more about the BDSM lifestyle as her brother urged. "Extras were a luxury, and I don't mind going without."

Glaring at the ogling saleslady, Vicki shoved her hand down farther. Her index finger lodged between his cheeks, the rest of her hand cupping his buttock. Jesse quivered beneath her grip but otherwise didn't move a muscle, while the saleslady flushed even darker and finally whirled to disappear down a side aisle.

She tried to keep her voice firm instead of sultry, but her voice sounded like she'd slugged a flask of Jack Daniels. "I thought we agreed to no flirting."

"Um, it's your hand down my pants, ma'am."

She couldn't help leaning into him, squeezing firmly, letting him feel how strong her hands were. She'd grown up on a ranch and although she had two older brothers, her parents had always believed in hard work for every single person in the family. "What did I tell you to call me?"

"I can't." He breathed short and fast. "If I say your name while you're touching me like this, I might not be able to control myself."

His erection throbbed against her stomach. Closing her eyes, she fought off the urge to slide her hand around to the front of his pants instead. *Not here, not now. Get a grip, Vik.*

She gave him one last squeeze and slowly pulled her hand up out of his jeans, but she slid her palm higher, up beneath his shirt along his back, stroking less private skin. "I can't seem to stop touching you."

"I'm not complaining."

Of course her continued stroking did nothing to ease his discomfort, and they certainly couldn't walk around the store like this. Reluctantly, she pulled away to give him some space. "Let's get out of here. I need to see Victor right now."

"Your brother? But I'm not ready for an interview. I should change—"

"Not your interview." Her mind whirled, as unsettled as her stomach. Jesse needed her to be in control, but that's the last thing she was thinking about right now. *I have to get help before I do serious damage to him out of ignorance.* "This is for me."

Chapter Seven

From the moment Jesse walked into the plush offices of VCONN Tower, the power and presence of the company's CEO bore down on him like a semi-truck barreling down the freeway at top speed. Vicki paused at the trophy case and fondly recounted some of her brother's great football moments. The pictures revealed a dark-haired man with stark, harsh features. His cheekbones were sharp and unforgiving. His eyes burned with the fierce light of desire to beat any and all competition.

The oppressive weight of the CEO's power only increased the higher they went toward his office. By the time she chatted briefly with the secretary and asked if her brother was busy, Jesse was lightheaded. The man's presence was suffocating him. How could he possibly meet him and expect to work here? Especially if Vicki wasn't here.

I want to be where she is, not here.

The shiny black door swung open and the man himself strode out with a large smile on his face that did little to diminish the rolling wave of power that swept before him.

Jesse fought to keep himself calm and unaffected, but damn, the man was a walking explosion of danger just waiting to happen. He didn't want to embarrass her by fainting because he was terrified of the Master. Even if she hadn't told him her brother was a sadist, Jesse would have known. Victor

Connagher was a sleek predator, a man who delighted in exploiting his opponent's defensive weaknesses, whether on or off the field.

Like a predator, he caught a whiff of Jesse's fear and a threatening growl rumbled from his chest. It was all Jesse could do not to drop to his knees and wrap his arms around Vicki's legs, pleading for her protection.

"V!" Vicki hugged her brother, oblivious—or immune—to the danger. "Rachel said you were busy. You didn't have to drop everything to see me."

"You know I'll drop everything for you, Little V. You're always welcome at VCONN, and I've been meaning to call you anyway. Shiloh has come up with some great ideas to help launch your fashion line."

Little V. Jesse shuddered. Yes, she carried the same power as her brother, whether she knew it or not. Maybe she wasn't a sadist. Maybe she wouldn't delight in his pain. But she would love to conquer him. If she'd only let herself begin, she'd raze him to the ground in a heartbeat.

I can't wait.

"Who's this?"

Jesse didn't look up to meet the man's questioning gaze. He was too afraid his knees wouldn't hold.

She reached toward him, and he seized her fingers, moving closer to her side now that she'd made the first move. "This is my friend, Jesse. Jesse, this is my oldest brother, Victor. Our middle brother, Conn, lives in Missouri."

Now Jesse dared to lift his head and look into her brother's face. Victor's eyebrow shot up, a thousand questions burning in his dark gaze, but he shook Jesse's hand, a firm grip but not punishing. No, that was for Vicki, if she ever wanted it.

Her brother knew exactly what he was looking at. Victim. Prey. He had to wonder exactly what Jesse was doing with his precious sister. Why she'd stoop to touch a guy like him. Especially when she had a man like Reyes at her beck and call.

Vicki wasn't one to beat around the bush once she'd made up her mind. "I need your help."

"So I see." Victor sat down behind his desk. "Where'd you meet Jesse?"

"It's a long story."

Victor kicked back in his chair and propped his ridiculously ostentatious cowboy boots on his desk. "I'm all ears."

She filled him in on Jesse's background, how she knew him, and the snowstorm that had brought him into her house. "Honestly, I had no intentions of letting him stay with me for more than the night. I wasn't thinking about taking him in permanently, not at all. It just...happened. I couldn't leave him on the streets, and now that he's safe, I can't stand the thought of letting him go back."

"Wait a minute. You said permanently. Are you thinking about *keeping* him?"

"You make him sound like a pet," she grumbled. "All I meant to do was get him a job, help him get on his feet and then go on my merry way."

"And now?"

"He's only been at my house two nights, and I can't..." She dropped her gaze to her hands. Her knuckles were white, her fingers turning red from the fierce grip she kept on her emotions.

"You can't what, Sis?"

Her cheeks burned. "You're my brother, V. The last thing I want to do is tell you all the things running around in my mind every single time I look at him. You'll probably beat him up or something."

"Nah," he drawled. "That's Conn's department, not mine. Mama might horsewhip him though."

Vicki jerked her head up and glared at him. "Nobody's going to lay a finger on him, do you hear me?"

"Protective, aren't we?" He gave her a sardonic smirk that made her grind her teeth. "What do you want me to do, Sis? Give him a job? It's done."

She blew out her breath in a loud huff. He knew damned well what was eating her, and he was going to enjoy every minute of it. He was playing games with her, just like he'd done when they were kids. Part of the fun would always be making her ask. "I thought that's all I wanted you to do, but things have changed. Now that he's in my house, I want him." When her brother's eyebrow shot up higher, she quickly added, "To stay. I want him to be safe."

"And you want him." She opened her mouth to deny it, but he put his feet down and leaned forward, all teasing gone. "You came to me for help because I'm a Master, not because I'm your brother."

Miserably, she nodded. Tears burned her eyes. "It's so complicated, V. I didn't know it would be this hard. Once I saw him, I couldn't leave him, and now, I don't want him to leave. I'm afraid I'm going to lose Elias, but I want to take care of Jesse too. Mostly, I'm scared that I'll end up taking advantage of the situation."

Victor came around before his desk, sat on the edge, and took her hands. "I suspected for a long time, Sis, but I didn't know for sure. Is Jesse the first man who made you feel this way?"

She nodded, determined to get all her angst out before she thought too hard about what she was telling her brother. The same person who'd made it impossible for her to date anyone as long as he'd lived at home because all the boys were scared to death of him. "He's been abused and he's had a terribly hard life. He came to me for help, and I don't want to make it worse for him, but I can't stop touching him. The last thing I want to do is screw him up even more."

"Don't make the mistake of thinking Jesse is submissive because of his life on the streets. I'm not a sadist because I was tortured or because Mama and Daddy had a private version of the *Texas Chainsaw Massacre* at the ranch. That's a load of crap and it always pisses me off when people assume we must have been abused or 'ruined'. I was born this way. You were born this way. Jesse is a born, natural submissive, and he proved himself to be a survivor. He can certainly survive you. In fact, he'd like nothing better than to survive whatever you can do to him."

"Who'll protect him from me?"

"You will." Victor gave her hands an encouraging squeeze. "You've already protected him by seeking help. I've been waiting all these years, afraid to push you, afraid to ask too many questions, but I knew when it was time, you'd know where to go."

"Did you have this talk with Conn?"

"Sure did. And he had this talk with me when I first met Shiloh." He hesitated, his eyes narrowing on her face. "I had this talk with Mama too. You really ought to be talking to her and not me."

But Vicki was already shaking her head. "Are you insane? I can't get Mama to agree with me that the sky is blue. What am I going to do, call her and say, 'Oh, Mama, by the way, I took in a homeless man and I'm going to keep him.'"

"Sure."

The thought made her stomach churn. "Never in a million years. I'd rather talk to you. Why not Mal too?"

His producer and friend, Malindra Kannes, had created several risqué shows for VCONN, and as a result, was known as the Mistress of Dallas. "Mal would be glad to help you, especially if you think you might be into punishment."

Pulling her hands away, Vicki covered her eyes and tried to calm the fire blazing across her cheeks. "I have no idea. I don't know why it's happening. Why now and not years ago?"

"Because you found *him*. All his life, he's been searching for the place where he'd belong, exactly as he is. He wants to belong to you."

"You could tell that from meeting him?"

Victor ticked the signs off one by one. "He couldn't meet my gaze until you took his hand."

"He was nervous—"

"He stepped as close to you as he dared." Victor ignored her interruption. "He silently begged for your protection while also sending a message to me that he was taken. You told him to wait for you, and he sat where indicated without a single hesitation, eyes only for you, his body tuned to you. I bet that when you touch him, however innocently, he sinks immediately into submissive invitation. Eyes down, shoulders and body relaxed, eager and willing to do whatever you tell him, and I mean anything."

"How did you know?" Her voice sounded hoarse to her ears. "Is it that obvious?"

He laughed softly. "Yes, to me, to anyone who knows how to read the signals. What does Elias have to say about this?"

"He's tolerant, but also jealous. I don't know how we're going to work things out. We'd sort of broken up, but he's back in my life now that Jesse is with me. I called him to run a background check the first night, and he went ballistic."

"I imagine so. Look, Sis, I'm the last person who'll ever judge you. If you want to keep both of them, you'll figure out a way. You said yourself that bringing Jesse home brought Elias back. Maybe it's meant to be."

Mentally, she had to pick her jaw up off the floor. "I never thought you'd tell me to... I mean, it's two men, V. *Two.* I can't get my own mind around the logistics. Elias and I talked every once in a while about marriage, but he's a cop. You know how dangerous his job is and the shitty hours he puts in. He's already been through one divorce. I know he loves me, and I love him, but I don't know that we could actually get married and not kill each other, even if the drug dealers don't shoot him down on the street."

"I will never say a word against Elias or Jesse or both. However, I will admit that I was worried about you each time I saw you and Elias together. You're both so hard and fierce, so Dominant, whether you play any sort of games in the bedroom or not. You're too much alike, and neither one of you will back down from the challenge or argument. I suppose that's why you two broke up?"

She nodded, trying to swallow the lump in her throat. "You don't think I'll ever be able to work out a long-term relationship with him?"

"I never said that. In fact, you may have the answer sitting outside in my waiting room, if you can get Elias to accept him. First, though, you need to take care of Jesse. In his mind, he's already given himself to you. It's up to you to protect him, even from Elias, and especially from yourself."

"That's what scares me to death." She blew out a shaky breath. "I don't want him to feel like he has to get a job and leave, but I don't want him to feel beholden to me, either. I don't want him to stay and put up with me and Elias's shit because I helped him."

"I can recommend a therapist who specializes in complicated BDSM relationships. You should both see her, immediately, before you get involved in an intimate relationship. Elias too. If he's serious and committed to working out a life with you, then he'll go."

"Definitely. I'll do whatever I need to do to make sure I don't mess this up. Elias..." She shrugged. "I don't know. When I feel better myself, I'll have a talk with him and we'll go from there."

Smiling, her brother leaned down and hugged her. "You're quite a woman, Beulah Virginia Connagher."

"Why'd you have to go and call me that? I thought you were going to help me!"

Victor laughed. "You can always call me, Sis. You can call Conn too, although his advice usually involves a poetry quotation. I hope you paid more attention in English than I did."

"I'm surprised you didn't use any football metaphors."

"Ah, I've been remiss. Let's see, Jesse is on your team. You have to call the plays and lead the team. He depends on you to tell him exactly what to do, but he'll run anywhere on the field, just because you told him to go. Your whole season is on the line, and if you call the wrong play, somebody might get hurt.

Jesse will run for you until he drops, and if you can get the ball to him, he'll sacrifice his own body to the defenders in order to catch it. He'd rather die than let you down."

She groaned. "Is Elias on the field too?"

"Of course. He's the linebacker trying to sack you for a safety."

"I've been tackled once—even though we were playing flag football—and it wasn't pretty. I don't think I like this game, V."

"Yeah, I remember when that punk slammed you to the ground, even though the ball wasn't anywhere near you. What happened to him on the next play, Sis?"

"You and Conn both smoked his ass."

Victor smiled and goose bumps raced down her arms. She suddenly wondered if that was the toothy smile that Elias saw on her face. "If you ever need help tackling Elias, call me. I'll leave Jesse up to you."

Chapter Eight

As soon as she stepped outside into the waiting room, Jesse shot to his feet. He rushed toward her, hovering close but hesitating. *As though I might rebuke him.* She wrapped her arm around his waist, and he collapsed against her, his shoulders shaking.

She rubbed his back in gentle circles. "What's wrong?"

"Please don't send me away!"

"Of course not. That's why we're here. Victor's going to help me so I can take better care of you."

"He didn't tell you to get rid of me?"

Victor let out a low, rumbling chuckle. "I expected you to know Vicki better than that, Jesse. If you tell her to do something she doesn't want to do, you'd better have a good head start on her."

Clutching her tighter, Jesse didn't laugh. Throat aching, Vicki pressed her cheek to his. "Nobody's going to take you away from me unless you want to go."

He drew tighter, vibrating with tension, pressing his body against hers desperately, because Victor had stepped closer. Victor reached out and gripped Jesse's chin, forcing his head up to met his gaze. She had to bite her lip to keep from jerking

Jesse away protectively. Victor knew exactly what he was doing, not fumbling around in the dark like a scared novice.

"My family is the most important thing in the world to me. If you're hers, then that makes you mine too." Smiling at the stunned look on Jesse's face, Victor released him. "She'll protect you, and I'll protect her. There's no reason to be afraid of me, because she'll tack my hide to the side of VCONN if I even think about hurting you. Welcome to the Connagher family, Jesse."

He straightened, his eyes flaring with surprise. "What?"

"She told you to call her if you needed help. So now you can call me too." Victor offered a business card. Hesitantly, Jesse reached out to take it, as though he thought her brother might snap his head off. "That's my personal number. Tomorrow, we'll sit down and talk about what kind of job you may want, although..."

Dark eyes gleaming, Victor turned to Vicki and she groaned out loud. "I know that look, V. What are you thinking?"

"Let's go upstairs and talk to Shiloh. I think we might be able to do something very interesting indeed to launch your line."

"I don't even know what I'm going to call it yet." She kept her arm around Jesse's waist as they walked out of Victor's office and headed for the elevator. Nobody looked at her strangely, least of all her brother. It simply felt so good to touch Jesse, to feel him against her side and see the light in his eyes every time he looked at her. "I still need to design the signature gown. I had a new idea for Jesse today, but I never planned to include men's wear."

Victor opened the door to his penthouse suite and waved them inside. "That actually fits into what we've been talking about."

"What have we been talking about?" Shiloh Holmes—soon to be Connagher—rose as they entered the main living room.

It was impossible not to smile when Shiloh entered a room. She brightened the area around her and lightened everyone's spirits, but most of all, Victor's. The hard edge of gloom in his eyes that had made Vicki worry for him so much had softened into the same kind of glow that came into Mama's eyes anytime she talked about Daddy, even though he'd been gone for years.

"Your idea for building interest in Vicki's line."

Victor took his fiancée in his arms and kissed her with so much passion that Vicki had to turn away for a moment. Unfortunately, she turned toward Jesse. As though he felt the power of her gaze, he whipped his head around. His eyes gleamed, deep, inviting pools of blue-green. She started to drown in conflicting emotions. Desire. Worry. Fear. Her heartbeat thudded in her ears and she swayed, unconsciously pulling him closer.

At Mal's booming hello from the hallway, Vicki jerked back, her cheeks heating. She couldn't even seem to control herself in front of other people. Meanwhile, Jesse took one look at the statuesque black woman and darted behind Vicki. His palm burned through her shirt, heating her back.

Mal took one look at the man hovering at Vicki's back and a huge smile broke across her face. "I knew it." She hugged Vicki and gave him a slap on the shoulder. "Good for you, hon. If you need help housebreaking him, you give me a call."

He muttered beneath his breath. "I'm not a dog."

With a low, wicked laugh, Mal stepped around her and leaned in close to Jesse. "If I tell you to heel, you will."

He tipped his chin up and broadened his stance, but he didn't take his hand off Vicki's back. "No, I won't. Not for you."

A sharp thrust of emotion tore through her. Rage, jealousy, she wasn't sure. All she knew was that she didn't want Mal touching him, or Jesse doing anything for her. She moved closer to Jesse, putting her body between them. "He's mine."

"Of course he is, hon," Mal drawled, not at all fazed by the sharpness in her voice. "But do you know what he likes? Can you take care of his needs, whatever they are?"

She started to open her mouth, but Mal cut her off.

"If he needs you to put a collar on him, strip him naked, and force him to sleep on the floor at your bedside, can you do it? If he needs you to pick up a paddle and whip him until he can't sit down, will you do it? And that's just getting started."

Vicki felt him hovering at her back, nervous, yes, but terribly eager, his muscles tight, his heat rising until her own shirt stuck to her skin. Her stomach churned with anxiety. Her mind felt jammed full of images: Jesse naked, bound, begging, helpless, crying, screaming...*for me.*

A shudder wracked her shoulders. "Do you need stuff like that?"

He pressed his face against her neck, burying his nose in her hair. "I don't know."

But his erection burned like a steel rod against her ass.

She lifted her gaze to Mal's face, thoroughly prepared for a smug I-told-you-so look, but the other woman only nodded solemnly. "People think it's all fun and games being a Dominant, but it's not. We have a huge responsibility not only to keep the submissive safe but to also learn what they need and then, we have to *provide* it, no matter what that need requires. It's your job to help him find out what he needs. You have to push his limits, explore his fears and his desires, and those desires will not always coincide with yours. If you care about him, you'll make sure he gets those needs met. Your boy

91

claims he doesn't know what he wants, but I guarantee he's got a few things in mind that will knock you reeling, and you haven't even gotten started yet."

Shaken, Vicki turned her attention to her brother, checking to see his reaction. He nodded as solemnly as his friend, his eyes dark and grim. "When I first met Shiloh, she scared me shitless."

"Aw, poor baby." Shiloh turned away from her glowering Master and offering a hand to Jesse. "Let's all get comfy before we scare the big bad Dominants too much. By the way, are you a model?"

He took a hesitant step toward the other woman, but stopped to check Vicki's reaction. "No, I'm not a model."

She tried to smile for him, but her lips felt too tight and cold. He sat beside Shiloh, who pulled Victor down on the sectional beside her. Jesse nodded and answered whatever questions they asked him, but he kept an eye on Vicki. She had a feeling that if she tried to sneak out of the room, he'd throw himself in her path and wrap his arms around her legs.

What the hell have I gotten myself into?

"More fun than you can possibly know right now," Mal said. At the look on Vicki's face—she hadn't meant to say anything out loud—Mal laughed. "You're scared right now and rightfully so. We've all been there. But the way that boy looks at you... Honey, you're going to have a wonderful time exploring each other's limits. He'd cut off his own dick if you told him it offended you."

"I don't want that kind of responsibility."

"Too bad," she replied in a breezy voice, locking arms with Vicki to lead her over to the couch. "You've got responsibility in spades now. I've got a package of literature I've been saving up in case you ever called. We can stop by my office on the way out. Besides, you've got nothing to worry about, not with the best Mistress and Master of Dallas sitting here ready and willing to answer any question you can possibly throw at us."

"Later." Shiloh sat forward, her eyes bright with excitement. "Jesse's agreed to do a commercial for you on VCONN."

"What?" Vicki narrowed her gaze on him. "I don't like that idea."

He paled, but Shiloh snorted, unworried about her hesitation. "He's gorgeous, Vicki. Why on earth wouldn't you use him?"

"That's exactly why. I don't want to *use* him."

Everybody looked at each other for a few seconds and then burst into laughter.

Victor fought to contain the grin twisting his mouth. "That's sort of the point, Sis."

"Use me." Jesse ground out, his voice harsher than usual. His eyes glowed with heat and Vicki forced her gaze to remain locked on his face and not wander lower. "I'd love to help you in any way I can. Shiloh has a great idea to promote your line, and it's something I can do for you. I want to do this so bad. Please, Vicki, use me. *Please.*"

When he begged like that, a warm ripple of desire crested inside her. She took a deep breath and concentrated on pushing that need away. "I haven't even heard the details yet."

"I've received at least three calls a day—and up to as many as ten or more—since I wore your gown at our premiere of *America's Next Top sub*. So, build on that interest. Build on the success of our show and create a very hot commercial in that theme."

"My line is for professional business women. You know, stuff we could wear to the office, not..."

"Latex and leather?" Shiloh smiled, not offended. "Look, I get what you're saying. I don't wear BDSM to work, either, and I work for the sexiest cable channel in Texas with the meanest Master at its helm. Think about that dress you created, though. How sexy it was without being blatant. Nobody knew that the unusual back had been designed specifically because Victor likes to leave his V on my back. Nobody knew his marks were hidden beneath the material, until he chose to give them a peek."

"And look at yourself, hon," Mal said. "Ever since I've known you, you dressed like a lawyer. Conservative and stylish, but with a little flare that said nobody had better take you for granted. Nobody at your firm suspected you might be a Dominant, but we did."

"I still don't know why you could see it and I had no idea."

"Didn't you?" Victor kept his voice soft, but his eyes drilled into her, demanding the truth in that annoyingly protective— and right—big brother way of his. "You never felt like something was lacking? You weren't bored by the standard dating scene? Even with Elias, didn't you wonder why you two had to fight so much, even in the bedroom? Because don't tell me you two were slow and tender lovers."

She tried to be nonchalant, but she was afraid her emotions were as transparent as a window sheer. "I can be tender."

"So can I, but it's usually after I've used my riding crop on Shiloh. What do you need before you can be tender, Sis?"

Vicki stared at him and hoped she didn't look as stricken as she felt. Her heart hammered and sweat tickled between her breasts. *Making love to you has always been like wrestling a hungry crocodile.*

"That's for her and Jesse to figure out, later," Shiloh said firmly. "Right now, we need to define the angle for the commercial. Do the other items in your line have a sexy or BDSM component that we can flirt with?"

"Not really." Vicki rubbed her temple to ease the pressure. Stress headaches were a bitch, and right now she had so many worries and ideas crowded inside it felt like her skull was going to explode. "The gowns are all sexy, and even the business wear is stylish with a twist, but BDSM? I wasn't thinking about that angle at all. Sort of like my life, I guess. I was too busy being a professional business woman to think about anything else."

Gentle hands closed on her shoulders. Jesse had slipped off the couch to stand behind her. His long fingers kneaded carefully yet with enough power to remove the kinks from her muscles winching tighter as her blood pressure mounted from the stress.

She closed her eyes and sank into the exquisite feeling of having someone take care of her. Elias wasn't a touchy-feely kind of guy. Giving back rubs or holding hands while watching a zombie movie weren't things that would even occur to him. Touch by touch, Jesse was insinuating himself into her life, making himself indispensable. *Necessary.*

The thought probably should have scared her to death, but it felt too damned good to worry. She hadn't had to ask. She'd never have to ask for Jesse to do something like this, some small deed to take care of her and ease her burden, because he'd known, and he hadn't waited for permission.

Relaxing in the feel of this man's hands gliding over her shoulders, she saw Jesse dressed in the elegantly old-fashioned formal shirt with full sleeves and large cuffs. Remembering the way his eyes had gone dreamy when she'd mentioned her brother's collar, she mentally corrected the design by adding an elaborate cloth about his neck. Not a tie, but a cravat. One that she could take off.

One that I can tie him up with.

Her eyes flew open. "I've got it! Do you have a scarf I can borrow a minute?"

Shiloh disappeared into the bedroom and returned with a ladies scarf. "It's silk, which isn't ideal for bondage, if that's what you're thinking of."

Accepting the scarf, Vicki stood up and turned around. She didn't have to tell Jesse to come to her. He saw the invitation—the order—in her eyes. Immediately, he came around the couch and halted in front of her, his eyes bright.

"Earlier today, I had an idea for a shirt for Jesse. He's masculine enough to carry off a more delicate, fitted shirt in an antique style. At the time, I was thinking about a bit of lacy ruffle at the neck and wrists, with full, billowing sleeves, something like what a gentleman would have worn to a ball in the nineteenth century."

She turned up the collar of his denim shirt and wrapped the scarf around his throat and back around, pulling the ends back to the front and crossing them in a loose knot. "I'll look up some period knots and do something a little more creative than this, but you get the idea." Standing to his side, she gripped the material at his waist tighter against his body. "I'll take his measurements to ensure I give him a modern, fitted look—almost as if he were wearing a waistcoat instead of the loose, billowing linen shirts the gentlemen wore. I wasn't going to do men's pieces, but if I limit myself to shirts only, it may work."

Victor's eyes were narrowed and he drummed his fingers on his thigh. "Sorry, Sis, but I don't get it. Do you think straight men will actually wear shirts like this?"

Without saying a word, she pulled the scarf from Jesse's neck and started wrapping it around his left wrist. Eagerly, he offered his other arm, letting her bind his hands behind his back.

"A male Dominant could use the cravat to bind his submissive." Shiloh's voice had gone as sultry as a Texas summer day. "I'm not much into bondage, but I like this idea. You wouldn't wear something like that, V? For me?"

"For you, absolutely," Victor growled out in a rough voice that made her shudder. "Besides, I know how much you like vintage clothing."

"Whoa," Mal whispered. "Please tell me you have a dress I could wear with something like this built into it? Although I don't have a boy as pretty as yours to tie up right now."

The black-and-white zebra dress hovered in Vicki's mind. A little bit of red and black, braided together and then wrapped around the waist. "Yeah, I think I do."

"So we have your theme: professional daywear that conceals kinkier bondage," Shiloh said, her eyes bright with excitement. "Does that give you an idea for the name of your line, then?"

Vicki stared down at Jesse's hands. His breath came in short, fast pants, his head down and turned slightly, so he could see her reaction over his shoulder. She imagined him naked, his hair loose and tumbled in his eyes, his skin slick with sweat, bound to her bed so she could tease and play with him at will. The sight of the silk wrapped around his wrists sent a surge of visceral lust through her.

She wanted *her* ties on him, not a borrowed scarf. She wanted him... "*Bound.*"

"Yes," Jesse ground out.

"*By Vicki* doesn't sound right." Deep in thought, Shiloh drummed her fingers on Victor's thigh. "It doesn't have enough power behind it. What do you call her other than her name, Jesse?"

"Ma'am."

"That's fine and dandy for you two, but that's not enough for this," Mal said. "I don't suppose you see yourself as Mistress Vicki or even just Mistress V?"

"Not really," Vicki replied. "No offense, I just never thought of myself that way."

"Why not *Bound by Madame V?*" Victor leaned forward, drawing her attention to him. "That gives it a little more class. But you'll really have to think about this, Sis. Once you come out of the closet, you're going to get a lot of questions. Everybody will think they know your sex life, which can get downright hilarious sometimes."

She leaned against Jesse, dropping her head against his back to hide her face so she could think. This was all so new, strange and crazy. All she'd wanted to do was start her own fashion line, finally realizing a teenaged dream she'd given up ages ago. Instead of vague ideas about fashion, she'd committed to what she thought of as a real, grown-up career. It'd been crazy to work her ass off in college and fight her way up the ladder at the firm rung by rung, on the verge of a partnership...

Only to turn around and walk away from it all.

Whether she and Elias managed to work out things or not, she hadn't been able to bear standing on the opposite side of the justice system from him. She'd found the courage to just walk away from years of college and hard work and she'd never felt better, despite the stress and anxiety of starting her own business.

Then she'd decided to keep Jesse, even if that caused more problems with Elias.

Do I have the courage to go on television and show my face at fashion shows across the country as Madame V?

Jesse shifted slightly. His shoulder muscles moved beneath her cheek, a subtle reminder. He waited for her to decide what to do with him. She had this gorgeous man tied up, more than willing to do whatever she wanted. Could she turn her back on him? Leave him on the street standing in the snow, because she was too embarrassed to reveal the truth?

She pushed her face firmer against him, breathing in his warm scent. He smelled like coconut—the shampoo she'd left in the guest bathroom downstairs. She'd never thought it would smell good on a man, but breathing his scent made her mouth water.

Straightening, she ran her hands down his arms, lingering over his forearms and bound hands. "Let's do it. I like *Bound by Madame* as the line's name, and then I'll use the V from my name in my label. I want Jesse protected by contract, though. Can you set us up something, V? I want to make sure he gets paid whatever makes sense, at least VCONN's going rates, and he can walk away whenever he wants."

Jesse turned around to face her, his eyes glowing with intensity. "Me walking away from you is as likely as a blizzard in hell."

Smiling, she unwound the scarf from his hands. "Be careful, Jesse. After all, it was a Texan blizzard that brought you to me."

Chapter Nine

What the hell is she up to?

Elias shifted on her bed, trying to figure out what was taking her so long in the bathroom. Last night, they'd been too frantic to even make it to the bed for the first three or four times, and now she wanted him to sit here and wait while she primped.

God, I need a drink. A couple of shots of whiskey would take the edge off, mellow him out so he didn't fall on her like a raving lunatic. That's the only way he'd survived three whole months without her. And of course driving by like a lovesick fool to make sure her place was secure. Sometimes he'd even sat outside in the wee hours of the morning in his truck, just watching, remembering.

If he'd used his key and come to her one of those dark nights, would she have forgiven him for walking out? If he'd called, just once, instead of sitting in his empty apartment staring at the phone all fucking night?

Or did it take a half-starved, homeless kid to bring us back together?

The bathroom door opened, and Elias damned near choked to death because his heart tried to crawl up his throat. He couldn't breathe as Vicki came near her bed.

She wore a filmy, white negligee that tied beneath her breasts and fluttered about her hips, oddly demure but so damned sexy he couldn't remember his own name. Her dark hair fell loose and soft about her shoulders and her molten chocolate eyes shimmered in the candlelight. She picked up an opened bottle of wine on the bedside table and calmly poured two glasses of red. Still silent, she handed him a glass and sipped hers, watching him with those dark, mysterious eyes.

He tipped his head back and drained the whole thing, even though he hated wine.

"What do you think?"

It had to be a trick question. Narrowing his eyes, he tried to make a joke. "Did we get married and I forgot about it?"

Her eyes caught fire and she slammed the fragile wineglass down so hard he feared it might shatter. "I told him this was a stupid idea."

"Jesse?" Elias fought to keep an even voice. "What the hell does he have to do with...with...?" He swept his hand at her negligee, fighting not to fist his fingers in that transparent material and rip it off her.

"He swore you'd like it."

"So what, now you're letting your cabana boy pick out sleazy underwear and babydolls? For me?"

"At least I'm not wearing it for him." She whirled away. "Forget it, Reyes."

Jumping up, he whipped out his arms and caught her, drawing her back toward the bed so he could sit back down. She jerked away and fought his grip, but he wrapped his arms around her and held on until her ire faded.

When he saw the tears on her cheeks, he cursed beneath his breath and held her tighter. He'd forgotten that sometimes anger from her hid her true emotion: hurt.

"I never should have worn this thing. I hate it." She sniffed, a tiny little sigh of her breath, which in another woman would have been full-blown wailing and sobs. He tucked his head close to hers, even if she skull-slammed him. "I told him it was a stupid idea. Just forget it."

"How could you hate this babydoll when I'd like nothing better than to rip it off you and ravish you senseless?"

She shook her head, so he drew her harder into the cradle of his thighs, pressing her against his erection. "That doesn't mean anything. I bet you had a hard-on as soon as you walked into my bedroom."

"It wasn't this big, babe, this hard, this painful." He lowered his voice and nuzzled her neck. "I'd like to think that you might say 'I do' to me someday."

"You'd have to ask me first," she retorted.

She had him there. He'd thought about it, sure, even when she was still an attorney. Even if she had to stand between the law and the very criminals he was putting away. But then his bigger head had started working again and he'd remembered how quickly a marriage could go down the shitter when he worked his kind of hours. "I can't stop being a cop."

"And I can't give up Jesse." She whispered, but her voice rang like steel. "If you love me at all, don't ask me."

Not even for me? The words thundered in Elias's head, but he refused to voice them. He did love her, and he'd had his chance. He'd fucked it up and walked out three months ago. That she'd let him back in this far was more than he deserved. He had no right to demand her whole heart for himself.

God forgive him, she'd already given up her career. Maybe not for him, not in so many words, but he couldn't ask for anything else. It was his turn to sacrifice to be with her, and the only damned thing he had was his own fool pride.

His stomach churned like he'd swallowed a fist full of razor blades, but he said nothing.

Nothing at all.

Why couldn't he give just an inch? Would it kill him to say that he loved her?

Her heart thudded so heavily in her chest that she couldn't breathe. She wanted to double over and wrap her arms around herself and moan in agony. Why did she let him tie her up in knots like this?

Loosening his grip, he sat back on the bed, giving her space to withdraw. She curled her hand into a fist, aching to turn around and just belt him in the chin. But that's what she always did. When they argued, she fought, challenging, refusing to back down. Wasn't that their greatest difficulty?

Slowly, she uncurled her fingers. She wouldn't give him a fight. Not this time. *But I won't retreat either.*

He smoothed his palms up and down her arms, hesitantly at first as though he, too, expected her to whirl around and sock him a good one. His lips brushed her shoulder, his breath warm and moist on her skin. Her spine arched and her head fell back. They'd made love countless times, but she couldn't remember him ever being so gentle. So hesitant and unsure of his claim on her affections and her body.

Just as carefully, she turned in his arms to face him. Any other time, she probably would have shoved him flat on his back and attacked him, but she was on a roll tonight for trying the unusual. It felt strange to stand there between his knees and let him stroke her, the barest glide of his fingertips and mouth over her skin. Her entire body hummed, vibrating with sweet tension and arousal.

He slid his hand up her thigh beneath the filmy negligee and he groaned against her mouth. She'd taken Jesse's advice and gone commando. Nothing kept Elias from feeling her heat and desire.

"Here you are wearing this nightie he picked out for me. That's pretty fucked up, Vik. What does your boy get out this?"

Her cheeks flooded with color and his eyebrows climbed higher. He let out a rough, low laugh, sliding both hands up to her waist to lift her astride his hips. Still torturously slow, he slid inside her body, drawing a desperate moan from her throat. She wanted fast, hard, no thoughts, no talking, because she didn't want the truth to come between them.

Damn Elias's bloodhound cop senses, but that's exactly what he wanted. Truth. And the best way to get it was to drive her insane with need.

"Is he listening, imagining that you're riding him instead of me? Is he down there beneath us, jacking off?"

She shook her head wildly. "No, he's not."

"He's not imagining his cock is in you instead of mine?"

Air, she needed air. She opened her mouth and sucked in a lungful, but her face still felt hot and tight. "He's not jacking off."

"How do you know, Vik?"

"Because I told him not to."

She felt the slight jerk in his thrust, that telltale little hesitation that said she'd surprised him. Judging by the size of his erection filling her up until she couldn't think, he didn't seem mad. She dug at his shoulders, grinding her pelvis against his, trying to drive him harder.

Sweat slickened his chest, his breath rasping in his throat, but he didn't lose that fierce control. "What do you mean, you told him not to?"

"He..." This was so wrong, so weird, to be talking about Jesse like this, but she was going to explode into a million pieces. "He's listening. Waiting for me to come. But he won't touch himself."

"Why?" Elias growled, arcing up off the bed to push deeper into her without giving her that long glide that would push her over the edge. "Why won't he touch himself, Vik?"

"I won't allow it."

"So when he hears you scream..."

So close, she was shaking, trembling with the spiraling need. When Elias clamped his hand over her mouth and rolled her beneath him, she was too shocked to struggle. Especially when he slammed so deep she saw a thousand stars burning in her mind. Screaming beneath his palm, she shook with the force of her climax, but all she heard was a muted, strangled sound mixing with his deep grunt of release.

He shifted them both up deeper into her bed and she made no protest. Her mind was reeling. She'd told him about her little "arrangement" with the other man and he wasn't bellowing at the top of his lungs. He wasn't storming down to his truck and peeling away from the curb. In fact, he tucked her face into the curve of his neck and simply held her.

He smiled against her forehead, a smug curve of satisfaction that also echoed in his voice. "We'll give your boy something to hear in a bit. That one was for me alone."

Chapter Ten

Days and weeks blended together in a blur as Vicki worked to get her line ready for the commercial and the upcoming show. She lost count of the long hours she and her seamstress spent on the signature gown and the new men's shirts, but through it all, Jesse was there.

Not constantly, thank goodness—for she would have lost her sanity and succumbed to temptation long ago. Long sessions with the therapist Victor had recommended kept Jesse out of sight, and the work helped keep him out of her mind. She went once a week herself, even though she couldn't really spare the time with the show only weeks away. Some of the questions were hitting too close to home.

Why don't you like to talk about your relationship with your mother? What's keeping you from a committed relationship with Elias?

She knew on both accounts. She just didn't like to talk about it, which evidently was the whole point.

Speaking of Elias, she hadn't seen him in several nights because of a major drug case he was working on. He didn't even have time to stop by for a quickie or a shower, but he did make a point to call every day. Although absent, he was connected, unlike their previous separation, but his solid presence wasn't there to keep her attention occupied. His body wasn't there to keep her distracted, and her libido was set on a constant rumbling roar.

Even the work, while frantic and stressful, was welcome, because it kept her hands busy with something other than Jesse.

He stood still and quiet as she buttoned the fitted turquoise shirt up his chest, helpfully tilting his head back so she could fasten the high collar. Even while she tied the neck cloth about his throat, she didn't really let herself see him. When she finally stepped back and let her gaze take him in, she couldn't tear her eyes off him.

His eyes glowed like living jewels, perfectly set off by the color of the shirt. With his hair tumbled about his shoulders and the tight black breeches she'd borrowed from VCONN's costume department, he looked like a young well-to-do lord from the nineteenth century. Nipped in tight at his waist but long and full in the sleeves, the shirt managed to give him elegance and old-world charm without making him look too feminine.

And his eyes. Damn it. She couldn't escape his eyes.

He said nothing. He didn't have to. The results from his first trip to the doctor had been clean except for some kind of intestinal parasite he'd picked up, combined with general anemia and malnutrition. He'd gone back after a round of antibiotics, and he'd put on twenty pounds and cleaned up his stomach.

Nothing would keep her from taking him.

Nothing but sheer desperation to keep him at arm's length as long as possible.

She heard the therapist's calm, clinical voice in her head. *Jesse is fully committed to you and he articulates very clearly what he wants and needs from your relationship. He's not conflicted. You are.*

Swallowing hard, she stepped to the side and waved a hand at the full-length mirror. "What do you think?"

He laughed softly. "I don't even recognize myself. I never thought I'd wear silk let alone something handmade by the most..."

He allowed the words to trail off and didn't finish the sentence. He must have seen the ragged tension in her body language, reflected back a thousand-fold in the mirror. Dark and solemn, his eyes said what he couldn't voice. They spoke of need, agonizing need. Elias hadn't spent the night in nearly a week, but it wouldn't have made a difference for either of them.

Jesse needed something her lover wouldn't...couldn't...give either of them.

Shame knotted her stomach. If she wasn't such a coward, she'd be meeting his needs. He depended on her for housing and his job as her model, despite the five-thousand-dollar check she'd put into a bank account for him with the promise of a percentage of the shop's earnings going forward. More, though, he depended on her for his physical needs. Needs that no one else understood, let alone could actually satisfy.

No one but me.

She knew it. He knew it. Hell, even Elias knew it. Ignoring the vicious ache of need clenching every muscle in her body when she looked at him wasn't fooling anyone.

Least of all myself.

She turned away from those haunting eyes and pretended interest in the sketches he'd done for her on the high worktable. In the mirror, she watched his shoulders droop with disappointment. "Take off your clothes except for my shirt."

In a second, he snapped from despondency to desperate, boundless hope. Without a single question or hesitation, he stripped off the tight pants, taking whatever underwear he might have worn along with them. It took all her self-control not to turn around and gobble him up with her eyes. Instead, she clutched a pen in her hand so hard her fingers hurt. She still wasn't exactly sure what she was doing.

What she was going to ask...no...*tell* him to do.

That's what he needs most of all.

"Slowly..." She cleared her throat to loosen the tightness that was trying to strangle her. Still clutching that pen like a talisman, she sat in her wheeled office chair and faced him. Luckily, the shirt was long enough to give her a moment to collect her thoughts, because she had the feeling that once she saw him naked she was going to have a hard time remembering her own name. "Unbutton the shirt, starting from the top."

His chest rose and fell so rapidly she could see each fluttering breath. He lifted shaking hands to the turquoise silk. Leaving the tight, high collar bound at his throat, he worked the tiny buttons loose, each one making her breath come faster, her pulse thundering in her head. He peeked at her from the curtain of tumbled hair hanging in his face, and his eyes cut her to the bone. So much hope. So much love. And terror, yes, because he was so afraid that she'd come to her senses and run like hell.

She wanted to, oh, she did. She wanted to flee. She wanted to throw him up against a wall. Or fist her hand in his hair and drag him down to torment her with his tongue.

Clutching the arm of her chair with her left hand, she forced herself to watch the show he was giving her. Inch by inch, he bared his chest, the flat planes of his stomach, the line of slightly darker hair down his belly drawing her gaze inevitably to his groin. Framed in the turquoise silk tails of his shirt, his cock rose hard and painfully aroused.

He'd waited so damned long for this, and so had she. But staring at his obvious need, she still wasn't sure what to do. Her mind felt frozen. Her eyes burned, not with sadness or regret, but such need, her heart so heavy in her chest that it felt like boulders crushed her ribcage.

She jerked her gaze up to his face, seeking a clue, a hint to what he expected her to do. If he wanted humiliation or pain, she'd probably crack or burst into tears. Mal had said something about dogs, collars, leashes, whips and flails.

Some Mistress I'm making. God, if that's what he wants, I don't think I can go through with this.

Seeing the panic in her eyes, he dropped to his knees in front of her and pressed his forehead against her thighs. "Let me touch you, just a little." His whispered voice shook as badly as her hands. "Please, Vicki, please. You don't have to do anything. Just seeing the way you look at me is enough."

"No," she forced out. The roughness of her voice shocked her and made him cringe harder against her legs. Desperate, he clutched her, wrapping his arms around her thighs like she was his last hope. "No, it's not enough. You need more than me looking at you."

She released her death grip on the pen, letting it fall to the floor so she could fist her hand in his hair. None too gently, she jerked his head up. "And so do I."

Jesse closed his eyes a moment, trying to hold back the flood of emotion and need. He didn't want to terrify her with demands and hopes and fears, not so soon. She'd taken that first step, and he knew what it'd cost her. He knew she was scared. Odd, but he'd never expected he'd be the calm, confident one when it came down to their relationship. Not as the bottom.

It was liberating, though. He'd always been forced, the victim whether unwilling or not. He'd never had the opportunity to think about what he'd ask for, how he'd guide someone into getting what he needed while still taking the bottom, but that's exactly what Vicki gave him. It was like finding the pot of gold at the end of the rainbow, only to discover it also held every single hope and dream he'd ever had in his entire life.

"Can I ask for things, m—" He caught himself saying *ma'am* and changed it to, "Madame?"

Some of the rigid tension tightening her body against his eased. "Yes, please, absolutely. What do you need, Jesse?"

Fuck me, hard, right here, now, push me down on the floor and take me as many times as you want.

Shuddering, Jesse pushed those thoughts away. Soon, dear God, soon, but for now, he simply said, "Can I touch your breasts?"

She let out a low, choking laugh that nearly made him release right then and there. "That's all you want?"

He smiled, deliberately quirking his mouth to give her the dimples she found so tempting. "With my mouth? Madame?"

"Just Vicki." She gently ran her fingers through his hair. "Unless you like calling me that."

"Vicki." He leaned up closer, hovering over her breasts while his gaze flickered up to gauge her reaction. "Can I lick and kiss your breasts until I come?"

"Make sure the door's locked and the blinds are down. I should have checked before getting started."

Since it was almost ten o'clock at night, he was pretty sure no one would be stopping by other than her cop, but he jumped up and checked the door and windows anyway. He made sure to do it quickly, with enough energy and enthusiasm to cause the shirt to flip up and expose as much of his ass and groin as possible. He headed back to her but jerked to a halt, spellbound.

Vicki pulled her sweater over her head, tossed it on the floor, and then reached behind her to undo her bra. It wasn't anything fancy—black, a little lace, but not racy—but he'd never seen anything sexier in his life. He dropped back to his knees before her and closed his hands over hers. "Let me, please?"

Giving him a nod, she opened her jean-clad thighs to him, letting him slide into her embrace. He pressed his face against her chest, listening to the pounding of her heart. Breathing her scent. She held him, too, her hands gliding over his chest, sliding beneath the silk to rub his back and shoulders, but she stayed away from temptation.

Let me see how long it takes for her to grab my cock.

He knew as soon as she did, he'd be done. Just thinking about her hand on him was enough to make him jerk and throb, so close to release. Instead, he concentrated on her. The silken skin inviting his mouth, the sweet, sexy curve of her breasts beneath the scrap of bra, her lush, hot scent. It wasn't perfume, just her—warm, clean, slightly spicy, better than homemade apple pie. Home.

Burying her hands in his hair, she held him close and let her head fall back. A low hum of pleasure vibrated her chest beneath his mouth. He unhooked the bra but didn't remove it with his hands. He used his mouth, nibbling and gumming the lace over her nipple, dampening the material before letting it slip away to reveal her flesh. The feel of her hard nipple in his mouth made him groan.

Arching against him, she tightened her grip in his hair, driving him to take more of her into his mouth. He closed his teeth carefully, listening for the slightest sound of pain or hesitation from her. He liked his sex rough and dirty and tiptoeing down the line of pain and pleasure, but she might not.

He had his answer when she yanked him away by his hair...and dragged his mouth to the other side. He rubbed his stubbled jaw against her, then his lips, soft, his teeth, hard, his tongue wet, winding about her. He sucked her breast into his mouth, straining to take as much of her as possible.

Pushing against him, she forced more of her flesh into his mouth, thrusting like a man, and it felt like his bones were melting. Like she was inhaling him instead of the other way around, and he'd just puddle on the floor while she drained him dry.

She pulled his head back to let him breathe. Eyes wide and dark, she stared down into his eyes, shaken, aroused, he hoped. She wrapped her thighs around him, dragging him so close her jeans rubbed against him—rough, raw, heaven. If she'd taken him into her body, he would have died for sure.

"How close are you?"

A tremor rocked his body but he held his breath a count of five, ten, waiting for the surge to ebb enough for him to talk. "Very."

She flashed a wide smile, dragged his mouth up to hers, and wrapped her hand around his cock. Her tongue thrust into his mouth, claiming him. He shuddered, groaning on a climax that scoured his brain with sand. He couldn't stop. Another spasm rocked his body, another, until he was shaking, his face wet, and she held him in the shelter of her body, rocking him like a baby.

He thought he'd shamed himself by crying like a virgin, but then he realized she was crying too. The pit of his stomach sank to the floor.

He'd never ever forget that day in the park when she'd come to him, pale as a ghost, shaking and sick. He might not have known her full name or where she lived then, but he'd known that she was a formidable woman with a steel core and a heart as big as Texas. She didn't break down. She didn't cry and cling. She took names and whipped anybody's ass who was too stupid to get out of her way.

But for that one sweet afternoon, she'd let him hold her. She'd sobbed on his shoulder and told him about her cop's partner. Her terrible guilt, her fear that it could have been the man she cared about. Even though she loved someone else, Jesse couldn't forget that he'd been the one to hold her that day. He'd allowed himself to hope. Not that she'd take him in, nothing that grand. Just that she'd care for him too. He wouldn't have minded the streets for the rest of his life if she came to him every day.

But then she'd disappeared. It was like she'd given him a glimpse of heaven in her arms, and then she'd wiped his existence from her mind. In the cold lonely months that followed, he'd finally realized why.

She'd been ashamed of breaking down like that with him. For her, it hadn't been a tender moment of shared compassion and simple human need, a dream come true. It'd been a weak, stupid moment that she wanted to forget.

Now Jesse barely managed to stifle the agonized pleading threatening to bubble up out of his throat. If she regretted taking him tonight, he'd die. He couldn't breathe, terror shutting down his lungs, his will, his mind. *Please, dear God, don't let her send me away. Don't let her be sorry for giving me the best release I've ever had in my life...*

Combing her fingers through his hair, she let out a ragged sound that he finally realized was laughter. Not regret, and not even amusement, but a sound of joy that made his heart swell in his chest.

She bit her lip, and the flash of her teeth made his cock stir to life all over again. "I have a little problem."

Was that a blush stealing across her cheeks? Her eyes were tight, her lips compressed, and her pulse thumped in her neck. A quick glance down and he noted her nipples were still rock hard and swollen. She squirmed a little against him and he suddenly understood perfectly.

Relieved, he grinned and licked his lips invitingly. "I think I can fix that problem if you remove your jeans."

As if he knew she might hesitate if he didn't use some sweet persuasion, he rubbed his cheek against her breast. Already abraded and fully aroused, her nipples ached so hard she shivered. Currents of electricity burned through her body, tying her breasts to something else that throbbed unmercifully. She jerked open her jeans and he groaned.

"Yes, yes, let me taste you, Vicki, please. I'm going to die if you don't let me taste you."

Hot and wet, his mouth pressed against her stomach in an open, tongue-swirling kiss that had her squirming and lifting in the chair to shove her jeans down. Backing away enough to help her get the tight denim down her legs, he lifted each foot and untied her tennis shoes, handling her like a priceless museum artifact. She hooked her fingers in the waistband of her panties, but he gently nudged her hands away.

"Allow me. Please."

He looked up at her with those eyes gleaming like bottomless pools of sparkling water, and she knew he wanted more, so much more. He wanted an order, an affirmation that she accepted this pleasure from him. No, that she demanded it. Swallowing hard, she leaned back and clamped her hands on the adjustable arms. Too bad she'd chosen such an uncomfortable chair.

My bed would be much better...and way more temptation. More temptation than I'm ready for right now.

Clearing her throat, she managed to get out the words, "No hands."

"Yes'm." He grinned, a slow, welcoming curve of his lips that made her heart thump harder. "Might I suggest you stand long enough for me to work those panties off with my teeth?"

"I'm starting to regret wearing my usual, boring clothes." She grumbled, her cheeks heating. Somehow she'd never pictured getting hot and heavy with Jesse in socks and basic briefs. "You deserve stilettos and a babydoll like the one you picked out."

Sitting back on his heels as she stood, he simply gazed up at her with his heart shining in his eyes. "You're perfect just the way you are. I wouldn't have you take me any other way. This is real, Vicki. The real you and the real me. Finally, this is what I've ached for all my life but couldn't have."

He stared up at her, completely vulnerable, his eyes dark with need. She cupped his cheek, smoothing her thumb over his lips. She couldn't help but wonder how many times he'd knelt like this before a man, forced to service him against his will. Her hand shook, faltering. *I don't want to hurt him.*

"Make me give you what you want," he whispered raggedly. "Drag me exactly where you need me. You can't possibly take me too hard or scare me in any way, I promise."

His eyes fluttered shut and his mouth opened in invitation, his lips soft against her thumb. So she pushed her thumb into his mouth, gripping his jaw with her fingers. *Harder. He said he wanted...*

Shuddering, he moaned and clamped his mouth down on her like he'd suck her hand down and swallow her whole. His tongue worked the sensitive pad of her thumb, his teeth gripping her firmly. She started to pull back but he bit harder, pushing her deeper into his mouth.

Opening his eyes, he begged silently. *Take me. Use me. Please.*

She fisted her left hand in his hair and jerked his head back, tipping his chin up so high his neck must ache fiercely. Pulling her thumb out of his mouth, she leaned down and showed him her breasts without touching him more than her hand in his hair. He strained forward, pulling his own hair, but she refused to let him get his mouth on her. "That's not where I want your mouth right now."

He growled a little, showing he wasn't completely passive. He welcomed the pain on his scalp, just as he welcomed her show of force. She twisted her hand deeper until she gripped the back of his skull, and then she pulled his face into her groin.

Nuzzling her with his whole face, he simply breathed, heating flesh that was already so hot her legs shook. Teasingly, he gripped the material in his teeth and tugged, up, not down, adding pressure instead of relieving the hammering need.

"If you don't get to it soon, I'll be done." She panted, barely able to speak. "And you won't get a taste after all."

Immediately, he moved his mouth up on her hip, seized a mouthful of cotton, and jerked so hard something ripped. The sound zinged through her, and she had to help, shoving the material down with her free hand, twisting her hips against his grip. Aching, so hot, she had to blink her eyes to focus on him. He waited, again, looking up at the flesh he'd revealed.

"Show yourself to me." His roughened voice abraded her sensitive nerves as badly as his whiskered jaws had rubbed her breasts, but he still managed to make it sound like pleading. "Torment me with what I can't have until you give it to me."

Her heart was beating too fast, but a deliciously wicked pulse of lust shot through her. She'd started this for Jesse, never realizing how much it would turn her on too. Widening her stance, she propped one foot on the office chair, opening herself wide. "What, this? Is this what you want, Jesse?"

He nodded so hard his hair whipped her thigh.

She let her hand rest on her tummy, low enough her fingers teased the dark curls. "Maybe I should just see to this myself."

"No! No, please." He leaned closer, letting her feel his breath hot and frantic on her skin. "I'll make it good for you. So good."

It was all she could do not to drag him in and grind against his mouth. He'd enjoy it, sure, but he'd enjoy it more if she made him wait. *So will I. If it doesn't kill me.*

Dipping her fingers lower, she parted her outer lips, fighting to keep from stroking herself to bliss. So wet, it was embarrassing. Just the way he looked at her, waiting, kneeling, it was enough to make her quiver on the edge. He shuddered, breathing deeply. His mouth fell open in silent plea, so she gave him her fingers. He hummed out a low cry, the pressure of his mouth unbearable.

She couldn't wait any longer. Neither could he, evidently. Maybe he saw the climax rising in her eyes. He didn't wait for her wet fingers to tangle in his hair before burying his face against her. He nudged her so hard she almost toppled over. Grabbing at his shoulders, she held on to him and tried not to fall apart.

Climax rocked through her but he didn't stop and she wasn't inclined to push him away. Not when he traced her so gently with his tongue, learning every fold and curve. He didn't use just his tongue, though—he used his whole face. His lips slid over her flesh in nibbling, soft bites. His breath was a light caress, his stubble a rough one that made her clutch his head harder. He nosed deeper, like he was trying to rub her scent all over him, like he didn't care if he never breathed again.

Trembling, she fought to stay upright, gripping his hair, even throwing her leg over his shoulder instead of using the chair. He kept his promise, no hands, but he still managed to take her weight gently down to the chair without ever lifting his mouth.

Breathing hard, she sprawled awkwardly in the chair but she couldn't find the will to move a muscle. Spasms still rocked her, fed by his mouth. He lapped at her delicately, groaning beneath his breath as though he savored every last drop.

Loosening her fierce grip on his hair, she stroked his face, silently trying to tell him he could stop. He looked up at her through his tumbled hair, eyes smoldering, as if to say, *Now that you let me here, I'll never leave.*

Still looking up at her, he latched onto her clit, sucking it into the heat of his mouth, firm, hard, and she exploded again. Panting, she finally gained enough sense to realize she was probably killing him. Her thighs were clamped around his head, one hand tangled in his hair, the other clawing his shoulder. She loosened her thighs' death grip and hauled him up for air.

"God, yes," he purred, draped against her thigh and her abused office chair's arm. "I could do that for hours, days, and never get enough."

She let out a shaky laugh and managed to get her watery limbs to cooperate enough to hug him. He nestled into her arms like a happy, adoring puppy. But all she could think about was Elias, which blasted through her pleasured haze with brutal intensity, leaving her stomach churning.

How am I going to tell him about this?

Chapter Eleven

"Hey, babe." Elias dropped his head back against his seat. "What's up?"

"You sound tired." The tone of her voice instantly set his senses on high alert. His Vik never sounded so timid and forlorn. "Bad day?"

"You have no idea." His gut burned like he'd swallowed acid. This was it. She was going to tell him not to come back—she'd settled her mind on Jesse. "That drug bust we've been working on all month went sour."

"Anyone hurt?"

"Not this time." He let the silence build, listening to her breathe. If he closed his eyes, he could see her beneath him, her eyes burning with desire. How could she want him so badly, but take the kid over him?

"Are you alone? Where we can talk a minute?"

He wanted to tell her he was busy, that his entire squad was hanging on his every word, but he couldn't lie. Not to her. He let out a heavy sigh. "I'm sitting in my truck in the 7-11 parking lot, trying to fuel up on enough caffeine to go finish my report on why we failed to nab our target. My new partner, Colby, is still in the office and I'm all alone, so you can tell me that you fucked Jesse and give me my walking papers."

"No!" She made a sound like a gasp. "That's not why I'm calling. Not exactly."

Narrowing his eyes, he wished he could see her face and body language. "What do you mean, not exactly?"

"I'm not giving you walking papers. That's the last thing on my mind." Her voice quivered, a slight break that made it hard for him to breathe for the ache in his chest. "I didn't fuck him. Not...exactly."

She paused, like she was trying to gauge his reaction. So he remained silent. Sometimes saying nothing was the best interrogation tactic of all.

"You know I'm working on a few new pieces for the show and he's going to model them for me. We talked about it, remember? That I'm sort of flirting with bondage and dominance elements? I asked if you were okay with that, because people are going to wonder what I'm into if I'm designing that kind of clothing."

Despite his heartache, he had to smile. Vicki never babbled. "Yeah," he drawled out. "I can hear the jokes at HQ now about how much you must like my handcuffs. But you know I don't care about that shit." *All I care about is you.* "You decide to try him out today?"

"Sort of." He heard a rustle, like she paged through papers, restless and nervous. "I finished his shirt and it looked incredible on him. Are you sure I can't make one for you?"

"Just tell me what happened, Vik. Did he come on to you?"

"He didn't say anything," she whispered so low he strained to hear. "He just looked at me. Like I was his whole world. Like he'd die if I didn't give him something, anything. A look. A touch."

Yeah, he knew the kid had that gobble-me-up-whole look that she found so irresistible. In all honesty, it shocked the hell out of him that she'd managed to put Jesse off this long.

"I had to give him something, Elias. It's been weeks since he moved in, days since you came over."

He shifted against the leather, growing uncomfortable in his pants. "Don't remind me, babe."

"I was so scared." Her voice trembled. If he'd been there with her, he would have drawn her into his arms, even though she was telling him what she'd done with another man. "He's so...so..."

"Needy."

"Yes. He needs so much. I didn't know how far he'd push me."

Elias hadn't smoked in more than five years, but he suddenly wanted a cigarette so badly he could taste the ash on his tongue. "So you asked him what he wanted. What he needed. What'd he ask for?"

"All he wanted was to touch my...breasts."

"That's all?" He forced out a laugh, despite the knife twisting in his gut. "Well, you do have mighty fine breasts, Vik. Did you strip him first? Of course you did. He needs to feel vulnerable, naked for you. What'd you think of his size, babe? Is he as big as me?"

"Thanks for the compliment." Now her voice would have stripped paint off the walls. Ah, there was the fiery steel core that he admired so much. "Yes, he was naked except for the shirt I made him. No, he's not as big as you. But you already knew that, didn't you."

"So I'm still your top dog, babe?"

"You know you are."

"Did he touch you, Vik? Did he suck those delectable tits?"

"Elias!"

He laughed at her shocked gasp. "Come on, Miss Priss, tell me all about it. How long did it take him to figure out how hard you like a man to bite and chew on those nipples?"

"Not long. Not long at all."

His balls ached and his erection threatened to bust his zipper. Loosening his pants, he sighed with relief. "I bet he didn't last five minutes."

"He lasted longer than you did that first night you came over."

Elias grunted a gruff acknowledgment. "I wasn't at my best because you made me sleep on the couch the night before." Unfortunately, he then remembered how turned on she'd been that night, how mad she'd been at him for finishing too quickly. Wondering what she'd done to get her own release, he felt his cock swell another couple of inches. "Did you take him to your bed?"

"No." She laughed, a dry, mirthless chuckle. "My office chair will never be the same."

Elias tried to laugh too but it sounded more like a growl. "Did you take him into your body?"

"No. Even when he was kissing my breasts; it was so weird, Elias. It was like *I* was inside *him*. I was possessing him. I *owned* him. I started wondering what it feels like for you to be inside me."

He swallowed to get some moisture back in his mouth and slipped his hand down to squeeze himself. "It feels damned good, babe. I like conquering you first and then sliding into you, staking my territory."

"Yes, that's what it felt like. Like I was *making* him take me inside, even if it was only his mouth. I wanted to be inside him, demanding and taking. I almost wished I were a man so I could take him for real."

He couldn't believe he was saying this, but he was so hard he'd surely lost half his brain cells. "There are ways, babe. You could get a dildo and use it on him."

He could almost hear her shudder. "No, nothing fake. For him, I want it real. I want to feel him."

He fisted himself, pulling his length through his hand, imagining how she would've pushed into Jesse's mouth, gripping his hair like he was giving her a blowjob on her breast. Christ, he almost lost it right there. "How'd you get off when he was done, babe? If he didn't come inside you, then I'm guessing you must have let him eat you out."

She made a low, strangled sound that he took for assent.

"How was his technique?"

"Good," she retorted in a rough voice. "Damned good. It's like he worshipped me, not licking or even kissing. He used his whole face, like he didn't care if he ever breathed again. Like his last wish was to die with my scent on him."

Immediately, Elias smelled her as though he'd rubbed his face between her thighs for hours. Remembering the way her body trembled and vibrated with her cries, her fingers tight in his hair, dragging him in to suffocate on that sweet, rich cream.

She let out a soft little tell-tale moan that made Elias's back arch off the seat. "Shit, get your fingers out of your panties, Vik. Are you trying to kill me?"

"Then stuff your dick back in your pants, Reyes. If you're going to come, then so am I."

Sitting up straighter, he turned the key in the ignition and backed out of the parking spot, but he didn't zip up his pants. "There's no way in hell this erection is fitting back inside my pants until I come inside you, babe. I'm on my way."

"You're too far away!" It came out as a wail, which made him smile as he gunned his truck down the road.

"Ten minutes, babe. I'll be inside you in ten minutes."

"I thought you had paperwork to do. Besides, HQ is at least twenty minutes away."

"Fuck the paperwork—it'll still be there tomorrow. Your neighborhood's 7-11 has the best coffee, so I always come here." He'd simply gotten in the habit of always coming to check on her first, and then stopping by 7-11 to sit and feel sorry for himself awhile before heading back to work. "Keep that engine purring for me, babe."

He could hear her breathing rasping louder, the hitch in her throat. "I don't know that I'll make it that long."

He floored it. "Five minutes, then. Are you going to take *me* to your bed, babe? Are you going to take my cock inside you?"

"Yes," she groaned out. "As soon as you hit the door."

"And when I come inside you, whose name is going to be on your lips?"

"*Elias.*"

Chapter Twelve

Vicki glanced uneasily between the men on either side of her as they walked into the VCONN Tower. After the office chair incident, she wasn't sure what to expect when Elias had insisted on driving them today for her commercial. So far, he'd been civil to Jesse, although not exactly warm and friendly. If she hadn't told him about what she'd done with Jesse, then she'd be dealing with wretched guilt, but for a second, she wondered if that might be better than this uneasy silent tension.

I've never lied to Elias. I'm certainly not going to start now.

Butterflies flocked crazily in her stomach. Shiloh had insisted that they should all personally be in the commercial. Especially Vicki. However, she'd never done any acting. Compound the BDSM flirting they were supposed to be doing with the possibility that Elias might be watching her play with Jesse on camera, and she was an utter mess.

"What time is Colby going to pick you up?"

Elias gave her a sardonic wink and even managed a smug look for Jesse over her shoulder. "About an hour, although he sounded like he was running late."

An hour. God. How much trouble could she get into in an hour? Way too much with Jesse at her beck and call.

She forgot her nerves once she started helping everyone pick out their clothes. Elias and Jesse went with Victor—she knew her brother was more than up for the task of keeping the two men from killing each other—while she took Shiloh and Mal into the ladies' dressing room. Just hearing the women squeal and ooh over their gowns made her glow with pride. However, she quickly noticed that her brother's fiancée wasn't her usual perky self.

Shiloh tried to laugh off her concern. "Oh, I'm just worried about meeting your Mama. We're supposed to take her to dinner tonight."

Vicki made a face like she'd just smelled something rotten. *Note to self: don't answer my phone or the door tonight. Vicki is looooong gone.* "Good luck with that."

"Oh, now, don't scare her to death," Mal said. "Between V's horror stories and now your obvious lack of enthusiasm, she's going to be thrilled to meet her monster-in-law."

"Sorry." Vicki shrugged uncomfortably. "I rarely talk to her."

Looking sumptuous in her red-silk gown, Shiloh laid her hand on Vicki's arm. "I'm sorry, hon. Did you have a falling out?"

"Not exactly." Vicki blew out a heavy sigh. *Only every single time I try to talk to her.* "V says we're too much alike. She has her way, I have mine, and we can't see eye to eye. I gave up discussing anything with her years ago, and I'm certainly never going to please her. The more I try to make her proud..." Throat tight, she shrugged and managed a lop-sided smile. "You know how mothers and daughters can be."

"I was close to my mom when I was younger—it's only in my adult years that I've drifted away."

"We were very close when I was a kid," Vicki replied. "She was a terrific mother. In fact, I'd decided before I hit high school that I was never going to have kids because there's no way I could be as good a mother as her when I grew up. Then..." She swallowed the flood of tears threatening to embarrass her. She always cried when Mama was involved.

"Don't feel bad, hon." Mal smoothed the zebra-print dress over her hips and gave a low whistle to her reflection in the mirror. "Most teenagers are pretty hard to live with. My mama said I went from the sweetest child to the most obstinate, independent, wrong-headed fool on the planet."

Vicki nodded along with Shiloh, half listening to their stories about the trials and tribulations of their teen years, but she didn't join in. The memory was too painful to share, too raw to drag out like dirty laundry for her friends to cluck over.

The past is the past, she tried to tell herself, but she couldn't get over it. In a heartbeat, Mama had gone from trusted confidante and friend to betrayal, and she couldn't forget it.

Maybe this wasn't such a bright idea.

Elias watched Jesse slip into his fine duds Vicki had made with such loving care. The poor kid kept peeking at Victor in the mirror and each time, edged closer to Elias. As though he'd protect him.

There'd always been tension between him and her brother. Part of it was the natural aggression between two very domineering sort of men. It'd be easy to get into a pissing contest, even though they might be family some day. Deep down, Elias had always suspected her brother really didn't like him much at all. Vicki's older, protective brother surely hated the fact that Elias was banging his sister without a ring on her hand. To compound his crimes, they'd split up, and he'd abandoned her when she'd needed him the most.

Or maybe that's my own guilt talking.

Between the junkyard Rottweiler and the sleek Doberman, the cream-puff poodle didn't have a chance. If Victor bared his teeth at the kid, Jesse would be under the chair, shivering.

"I'm surprised you're not going to be in the commercial with us," Victor said in a casual voice that didn't fool Elias one bit. Her brother might lord and master it over his employees but if he thought to bark orders at Elias, he'd find out that his bite was just as mean. "Vicki sent several extra shirts—hoping, I think, that I might convince you otherwise."

Elias snorted. "She knows better than that. I'm only here for moral support. Once she gets started, she'll be fine."

"Oh, I'm not worried about the commercial." Victor tilted his chin up and began winding the cloth about his neck that was supposed to be the bondage element. "Mama's going to stop by."

"What?" Elias shot to his feet and began to pace. "Does Vicki know?"

"Of course not," Victor drawled, shooting a smug look at Elias through the mirror. "Wild horses wouldn't have dragged her here if she knew Mama was coming too."

Worried, Jesse looked between the two men. "What's wrong?"

Elias rolled his eyes and blew out a disgusted breath. "Vicki doesn't exactly get along with her mother. It's like tossing two starving alley cats into a burlap sack when those two are in the room."

"So, what are you going to do?"

Surprised at the low, intent tone of Jesse's voice, Elias studied him. For the first time today, he met Elias's gaze steadily without flushing, cringing or dropping his gaze to the ground. He even narrowed his gaze and lifted his chin, his eyes challenging, as if to say, *Take care of her. Or I'll be more than happy to step into your place.*

Interesting. If Vicki's well-being was in question, Jesse would apparently rise to the occasion.

It was like a cattle prod shoved directly up Elias's ass. He'd assumed the kid was a total pushover, a little lapdog who'd yip his head off and then run the opposite direction when threatened, but he couldn't have been more wrong. He hated it when people made stupid assumptions and he'd just made a colossal one.

Tipping his head back, he laughed but without rancor. Maybe hell had frozen over, because damned if he wasn't starting to like this kid, even though every time he looked at Jesse he imagined that blond head between Vicki's thighs.

"What's so funny?" Jesse took a step closer, his hands clenched into fists. "I'll tell Vicki that her mother's on her way and we'll be gone in a heartbeat."

Elias gave him a friendly slap on the shoulder. "Thanks for reminding me that I can be an asshole."

Doubtfully, Jesse watched him like that friendly pat was going to turn into a right hook. "Doesn't Vicki remind you of that often enough?"

"Every chance she gets."

"So, what are we going to do? She's already so nervous about the commercial and the gala just around the corner, not to mention..."

Me. You. Us.

She had to figure out what she was going to do about them. Whether they could work out some sort of illicit arrangement without anyone getting hurt, especially her.

"I'll handle Mrs. Connagher if she arrives while you're filming the commercial." Although he found himself wishing he'd grabbed his bullet-proof vest out of the trunk of his car. "You help Vicki get this done as quickly as possible and maybe we'll be gone before Mrs. Connagher arrives. Otherwise, be prepared. She's never in a good mood after dealing with her Mama. She's likely going to rip our heads off if she even gets a hint that we knew her mother was anywhere inside the city limits and we didn't warn her."

Jesse pulled his hair back into a rubber band. "I feel like we're betraying her if we don't tell her now."

"I'm the one who called Mama." Until Victor spoke, Elias had forgotten her brother was even in the room. "Vicki needs her whether she knows it or not, and this stalemate of theirs has gone on way too long. They're both too proud to come together on their own."

Staring into the other man's dark eyes made even more alarming by the mask he wore, Elias suddenly realized he'd been very coolly and deliberately manipulated. Not only had Victor taken it upon himself to bring their mother into the picture to hopefully mend whatever rift was between her and Vicki, but he'd also managed to get Elias and Jesse working together like a team.

Well done, V. But damned if I'll ever tell him so.

Watching Victor and his girlfriend tape their brief interlude for the commercial made Elias feel like a damned pervert. They performed as though the cameras and people simply disappeared, and they were alone in their bedroom. In a smooth, unscripted twenty seconds, Shiloh deliberately antagonized her Master and let him tie her hands together with his cravat. Then he bent her over a desk. The red dress displayed her bare back perfectly.

The short vignette ended with a well-placed blow from his crop. They both wore masks, but everyone in Dallas who'd watched VCONN's hit show, *America's Next Top sub*, already knew that the CEO was a sadist. The masks would make the audience remember that thrilling first season and all the drama about Master V's identity.

Elias had never been a voyeur nor into S&M, but with Vicki standing beside him, he had to wonder. What was she going to do with Jesse? What sort of inclinations did she possess that she'd never told him? Had he been failing her in more ways than one this entire time?

Gripping her chin, he turned her head up to him. In typical Vicki style, she growled beneath her breath and tried to jerk away, but he held her hard enough his fingers dug into her skin. He searched her eyes, trying to delve for secret needs and desires, but all he saw was anxiety. "Show me what you want to do to him."

She tried to look away but he held her firm, making her meet his gaze. "I can't..."

"You can do this, babe." He planted a hard, quick kiss on her mouth. "Do it for me."

Jesse threaded his fingers through hers. Meeting his gaze, Elias gave him a subtle nod and the other man led her off for her final primping. Pale and halting, Vicki looked like they were taking her to the guillotine.

"Whoa, what sort of place have you brought me to?"

Elias turned as his partner joined him. "Hey, you're early. I'm not ready yet."

"That's cool." Younger and taller, Colby had the hard, mean edge to him that a man only gained in active military duty for his country. Two tours in Afghanistan made him tougher and leaner than most rookies. Just two years older than Jesse, Colby had him beaten hands down in experience and confidence. In a fight or shoot out, Elias would never doubt that his partner had his back. "So, what's going on?"

"Vicki's working on a commercial for her new fashion line. You might want to wait in the car—it's going to get rather steamy in here."

Colby's eyes narrowed with speculation. "Vicki's your girl and she's doing a steamy commercial with another guy. Why aren't you out there?"

Forcing a laugh, Elias shrugged. "She needs a pretty face for this. Besides, Jesse..." What could he say that wouldn't make him look whipped for allowing another man to play with his woman? Eyes tight and hard, Colby waited for his response, and he wasn't going to lie to his partner. "She's mine, but Jesse's hers."

Colby shrugged. "Whatever floats your boat, man."

Elias hadn't been paired with his new partner long, but after that comment, he wouldn't have traded him in for anyone else. He owed Colby big time. Which reminded him of one way he planned to pay his partner back. "Are we still on for Friday night?"

"I don't know." Colby sighed. "Wilson backed out. He claims his old lady won't let him play poker anymore, but I think he's just too afraid of pissing Rodgers off even more."

Rodgers had been a pain in Elias's backside for months. As a long-time veteran of the force, the man's transfer to their department should have helped with their backlog, not stirred up animosity and racial tensions. The only reason the guy hadn't been fired already was his seniority. In a few more months, Rodgers would retire. Until then, he took special delight in tormenting the youngest members of the force, which meant Colby had been on the receiving end of Rodgers's shit for months. Colby wasn't a tattletale sort of guy, so they'd decided to handle the man's venom with a not-so-friendly game of cards.

Rodgers had already been bragging how much he planned to fleece the "snot-nosed kid". But if they couldn't get at least one more neutral player, then even he might realize he'd been set up from the beginning. *Unless... Surely Jesse has learned a few tricks or two on the streets.*

"I think I've got our fourth player. I'll call you if he can't make it, but assume we're on."

"I don't think we've met," Mal drawled out in a whiskey dark voice that made Elias arch a brow in speculation. Damned if the cast-iron Mistress didn't sound like a purring kitty eyeing its favorite toy. "I'm Malinda Kannes, Executive Producer here at VCONN."

"Pleased to meet you, ma'am. I'm Colby Wade, Detective Reyes's partner."

"Oh, so you're a detective too. You used to be a soldier if that haircut's any indication. Have you ever done any acting?"

"No, ma'am." He gave Elias a look that said *what the fuck is going on?*

She squeezed Colby's biceps like she was measuring his arm for manacles. "So polite."

For all Elias knew, that's exactly what she was doing. *I hope she doesn't decide to measure his other equipment.*

"How would you like to be *my* partner for just a little while?"

Elias shook his head, trying to wave Colby off without drawing Mal's attention, but she knew what he was doing.

"Oh, don't pay any attention to him. He doesn't have any idea what kind of *fun*—" she squeezed Colby's arm again, hard enough that his eyes flared, "—we'll have."

Fuck being polite—Elias had to save him from doing something stupid. "If by fun you mean whips and shit. She's a Domme, Colby. A Mistress. She'll eat you for lunch."

"And what a delightful lunch that would be." The fierce woman somehow managed to pout playfully. "I don't have a partner for my portion of the commercial." She gave Elias a knowing smirk. "Miss Vicki is so attached to her young man that I doubt she'll share. It's only for the commercial, Detective Wade. You wouldn't leave a lady alone and desperate, would you?"

"That depends, ma'am." Colby's voice remained even and calm, but he stiffened, like a soldier braced for bad news. "What exactly do you need me to do?"

"Only this," she whispered, losing some of her playfulness. "Stand tall, defiant, insurmountable and tempt me to crack that firm resolve."

Elias had thought her fierce voice was scary, but this softness made his blood run cold. His partner stared at her for several long moments without replying. Surely he wasn't actually considering it. God only knew what kind of torture equipment Mal liked to use. Colby was too nice a guy to tell her to fuck off, especially on tape. He couldn't...

Colby gave her a thousand-watt smile of pure cockiness. "Sure. No problem."

Jesse wasn't used to people fussing over him. With a stylist yanking his hair and another powdering his face, he finally pushed up out of his chair and walked out of the room. *She* hadn't told him to stay, and he was sick of the waiting.

Vicki was going to play with him. In front of Elias. In front of the entire city. *I can't wait for everyone to see that I'm hers. Especially her cop.*

On set, he scanned the knots of people but Vicki must still be in the makeup room. Elias stood off to one side and by the tight, cold look on his face, he wasn't happy. Jesse hesitated, trying to decide whether he wanted to face that displeasure. Victor and Shiloh were on set with a man he didn't know, coaching him on his part with Mal.

Shuddering, Jesse moved over to stand with Elias. He definitely felt safer there than anywhere near the Mistress. Vicki didn't scare him, not at all, but Mal made him sweat, and not in a good way.

"Christ, I can't believe he's going to go through with this," Elias muttered, sparing Jesse a glance. "Would you go out there? With Mal?"

"Hell no. Who is that?"

"My partner."

Shit. No wonder they were shoving a mask down over the guy's face. Thanks to VCONN's infamous shows, everybody knew Mal was the Mistress of Dallas. If a detective on the DPD was doing a scene with a Domme...on television...

"Take your shirt off," Mal said in a rich, smooth voice that sent cold chills down Jesse's spine. She wasn't speaking to him or even trying to command, but the steel echoed in her voice. When she spoke, she was heard, and even an innocent request became a demand.

Colby simply arched a brow at her, either oblivious to that seductive power or so supremely confident that he bordered on stupidity. He didn't seem to have a submissive bone in his body. Why did Mal want to play with a lean and mean cop?

"What's the harm? You'll still have your pants." Smooth and rich, her voice teased with just enough daring and not enough command to send the cop running in the opposite direction. "Besides, in that button-up shirt and tie, you look like a detective or an office employee. That's not sexy enough for what we're doing here."

Colby glanced back at his partner and Elias shook his head. "Don't do it, man."

With a shrug, he loosened his tie and unbuttoned his shirt. "I'll strip down to my T-shirt but no further. I've got too many tats for people to recognize."

Mal's eyes smoldered even hotter and she wet her lips. "Nice. I hope you'll show them to me someday."

"Ready on set," Shiloh called out. "We just need a few seconds' worth, guys. Your set up is a dance club. Colby, all we need you to do is be reluctant but intrigued. Mal will do a little flirting and convince you to leave with her. We need the belt involved, Mal. Remember the dress and the message we're trying to get out. Fun, spur of the moment bondage, nothing serious. Right?"

"Right." Mal smiled like she was harmless. "Hit the music and let the cameras roll."

Slow rock with a heavy, pulsing bass began playing and someone flipped on a disco ball to cast sparkling lights across the set. Letting her body sway to the music, she turned away from the man watching her so warily. She danced alone, unafraid, not needing a partner on the floor, moving with a raw sensuality that had him staring at her with a growing hunger.

Even Jesse felt that subtle pull. Mal's sexual energy was magnetic, hypnotic, yes. But would it be enough to snag a man confident in his own sexual prowess?

Playing along, Colby stepped up behind her and settled his hands on her hips. They moved together, just a couple flirting on the dance floor. Mal didn't turn to him or try to take command of the dance. When his hands flexed on her hips, she agreeably turned in his embrace. She even snuggled her head up beneath his chin, letting him rock her body against his in time to the music.

From the sidelines, Jesse couldn't take his eyes off them. His muscles were tense, his heart pounding in anticipation. She'd make her move, he was sure of it, but when? How? So far she hadn't given any indication that she was a Domme strong enough to command even the most virile man in her bed. He'd bet every dollar he'd managed to save on the streets that Colby wasn't submissive. The man wouldn't take kindly to being made to look like a fool, especially by a woman. In front of his partner, no less.

He jerked hard enough that the swirling lights and shadows didn't obscure his movement. It was hard to tell what happened, but Jesse thought she'd probably bitten the man's neck. Hard, too, by the way he'd almost stepped out of her arms. Yet his hands dug harder into her lower back, pulling her tighter. Mal ran her hands down his arms, a slow rake of her nails that made Colby's nostrils and eyes flare with surprise.

Or growing lust.

He growled, low and rough. "What are you doing to me?"

She let out a husky laugh that made him tighten his hands threateningly. "Tempting you to walk on the dark side with me."

"You can't handle my dark side, honey."

Her mouth quirked and she reached up to cup his cheek in her palm. "Try me. You might be surprised at the darkness I'll find and how I'll handle it. How I'll handle *you*."

Holding his gaze, Mal took a step back and pulled the long braided red and black belt from her waist. She held it in both hands, lifting it so he could see it, still swaying her hips back and forth in time to the music. Teasingly, she reached up to drape it behind his neck. She pulled on it, bringing him down so she could brush her lips against his.

Jesse watched, breathless, sure that any minute Colby was going to refuse, laugh and walk away, or maybe even flatten her. His body vibrated with that kind of violence. Or maybe he was simply fighting himself. He palmed the back of her head and clamped his mouth down on hers, kissing her brutally in an extreme show of strength.

Mal even encouraged him, although she took his hand in hers.

So she could wrap the belt around his wrist.

He didn't pull away or raise his mouth, even as she tied his hands together in front of him. His shoulders bunched and corded. It was obvious that he could refuse if he wanted. He could have jerked his hand out of her grip or shoved her away, but he allowed it. Raising his head, he glared down into her face, eyes glittering, face dark, but he didn't walk away.

That's when Jesse understood what Mal had seen in the other man. She saw the *challenge*. Colby was a man who could physically and mentally refuse to bend to her will. If he chose to bend knee for her, it would be because he wanted to do so for her alone—not because he had to.

Some submissives melt at their Dominant's touch. Others fight because they want to be conquered. Mal would relish the battle of breaking Colby to her will.

She turned and walked off set without a single glance back. Hesitating a few moments, Colby jerked his shoulders back, head high, and strode after her with the intent of a man ready to do some serious damage.

Evidently he'll relish the battle too.

Elias cleared his throat. "Are you free Friday night?"

"Um, sure," Jesse replied, watching the man's reactions carefully. The cop's eyes were tight and guarded, but he didn't seem threatening. Surely he wasn't going to put a bullet in his skull and drop him off in the woods somewhere. "What's up?"

"Can you play five-card stud?"

Jesse let a slow smile spread across his face. "That's like asking a wino if he knows where the cheapest bottle can be found. I could play before I left home. Living on the streets, I learned to play for food. If I didn't win, I starved. Why?"

"Colby needs my help." Elias hesitated, his face as hard as stone. His throat worked, as though he fought to get the words out. "And I need your help to pull it off."

An olive branch, of sorts. A man like Elias wouldn't ask for help lightly, especially from the competition. But he wouldn't want a big deal made about it, either. Keeping his face smooth, Jesse shrugged. "Sure, no problem."

Who knows? Maybe I can actually prove to him that I'm not completely worthless.

Chapter Thirteen

"Oh, Vicki," Shiloh said, her eyes bright. "Your gown is incredible! It's going to look wonderful on screen."

Fighting back nerves after what seemed like hours in the chair while professionals styled her hair and face, Vicki gave a little twirl so the heavier floor-length turquoise skirt fluttered, revealing the sheer red layers underneath. A matching long red scarf wound around her neck, crossed over the turquoise halter-style bodice and wrapped around her waist to tie in a loose bow in the small of her back. She could use the scarf for bondage in the commercial, or the neck cloth on Jesse's shirt.

Assuming I don't hyperventilate first and pass out. "Thanks. It's not my usual style, but it's certainly eye catching."

"It's perfect for a fancy party, which is the set up for your commercial. We've got well-dressed extras scattered throughout the room with a bar we borrowed from another set. For this first shot, you're at the bar and Jesse will come up to you. You think he's hot, but blow him off and leave out the right-hand door. Don't worry about your lines—we'll add a voice-over after we're done."

"That's it?" She tried not to sound surprised...certainly not disappointed. So far, this was a rather clean shoot, nothing to do with BDSM or risky wear. "Seems rather tame for what I thought we were going to do."

Shiloh gave her a knowing grin. "It's the set up for what happens when he follows you. Don't worry—we won't be spending much time on this. Just look gorgeous and cold. Leave. Then we'll set up for the next shot."

Cold and untouchable she could definitely do. She sat down at the bar while Shiloh lowered the lights. Music played and the quiet murmur of voices started. Taking a deep breath, Vicki gave the bartender a nod. It was easy to pretend that she was back at the firm, the reserved, cold-hearted attorney just off a case, out for a drink or two.

Jesse walked up to the bar at her left elbow. Despite the cameras she knew were running and Elias watching in the wings, a surge of what could only be called lust blasted through her. Even in the darkened setting, his eyes glowed, the silk shimmered, and the low light glanced off his bound hair. He gave her a wide, hopeful smile. "Could I buy you a drink?"

She arched a brow at him and openly let her gaze run down his body. "No thanks."

Ignoring her words, he eased closer, ducking his head down closer so his breath fluttered over her bare shoulder, his lips a faint caress. "Are you sure? I'm up for anything you'd care to try."

His body heated her arm and the subtle touch of his mouth made her want to arch against him and purr. Her skin sparked to life, remembering every single lick and nibble of that delicious mouth. She lifted her mouth tantalizingly close to his and allowed a smug little smile curve her lips. "I'm sure."

Slipping off her seat, she turned away and glided toward the door, head high. With a sinking feeling in her stomach, she noted that Elias had left.

"Great job, guys!" Shiloh led them down the hall, talking over her shoulder. "This next part we're going to film in the parking garage. V said we could use his car."

Turmoil roiled in Vicki's mind, worry and nerves eating her alive. Elias had planned to stay through the filming. He'd taken half the day off just so he could be here this morning. Had an emergency come up? Or was it something else? Was he jealous? Had he been unable to watch her with Jesse? But they hadn't even done anything on camera yet, which only made her more worried.

Jesse took her arm, gently pulling her against his side. "What's wrong?"

Silently, she shook her head. It wasn't something she wanted to discuss in front of Shiloh. Besides, nothing may be wrong. He could have been called to HQ early.

"Elias's partner did a scene with Mal and she's got him cornered off set," Shiloh said over her shoulder. "I hope he knows what he's getting into. Mal looked like she would gleefully eat him alive."

So Elias hadn't left for downtown, not if Colby was still here. That pit in Vicki's stomach weighed heavier. By the time they made it to the basement garage, every butterfly she'd managed to forget had multiplied. She had to force herself to listen to the other woman's words.

"In this scene, you're getting ready to go home, and Jesse catches you. He's persistent, which annoys you. You decide to show him a little of what he's asking for, hoping to scare him off."

Vicki's palms were damp and her heart pounded so hard she started to get a headache. "Like what?"

"Anything you want." Shiloh winked, like surely Vicki had a hundred dirty ideas raring to go. "Just make sure you end up using your scarf or his cravat. Jesse, you come over here by me. We'll open with a shot of her by the car. Wait a minute."

That didn't sound good. Vicki turned around, half expecting to see Elias with his gun drawn or something equally dire, but the other woman merely frowned at her and V's red Camaro.

"The reds clash. V's car isn't going to work at all."

"We could use mine," Vicki said.

Shiloh winced. "I don't think a Mini Cooper is going to be dramatic enough, hon. I mean, look at you. You're not dressed for a Mini. You're dressed for an expensive, high-end night on the town."

"I meant my Jag. I've been keeping it here in VCONN's garage."

She led the way a few spots over to her silver Jaguar she hadn't driven in months. She'd lived that status-seeking, high-stress performance lifestyle for far too long. *That's a phase of my life that's thankfully gone forever.* "It's a leftover from my attorney days. It's too good an investment to ditch the car—I just didn't want to drive it around town any longer."

Shiloh whistled beneath her breath. "Perfect. Okay, give us a few minutes to set up over here and we'll get started."

She marched off to move the camera and lighting crew, leaving Vicki alone with Jesse, who immediately took advantage of privacy. "Are you worried about Elias?"

She nodded. "Did you notice when he left the set?"

"No. But don't worry about him. I know he's not mad or anything."

Arching a brow, she twined her fingers in Jesse's and pulled him closer. "How do you know?" He looked extremely guilty, which almost made her laugh. "Ah, you must have had a little man-to-man talk in the dressing room."

"You could say that. He wasn't upset at all, not like I expected. I think it's going to be fine, as long as you're fine with it." He let out a soft chuckle, but it sounded forced to her ears. "I mean, you can hardly look at me today, so I'm more worried about you than your cop."

She had to fight to keep from turning away from his steady, clear sea eyes. "You're right. It's just...awkward. I keep waiting for Elias to blow a gasket. I feel like I'm walking around on eggshells, which I hate."

Jesse leaned down so he could press his forehead against hers. "I know. I'm trying really hard to be patient and not push for more."

"But you want more," she whispered. "So much more."

A tremor shook his body. "Yes. But I'll wait until you're ready. I'll wait as long as it takes."

"What do you want? Exactly?"

"I'll show you."

Elias couldn't explain his sudden urge to be on set with them. One minute he was watching the relatively tame scene at the bar, and the next, he was in the dressing room, slipping on the black shirt she'd made. He didn't bother tying the neck piece, but left the shirt hanging open with the cloth loose like a scarf. He didn't know how to tie the damned thing anyway.

He caught a glimpse of himself in the mirror and hesitated. Everybody in Dallas would recognize him as the cop who'd done a sleazy commercial. He didn't care for his own reputation, but he didn't want to bring dishonor to the squad or his profession.

Luckily, Victor had left a spare mask beside the shirt. Grimacing at the man's arrogance, Elias pulled on a mask and hoped her brother didn't gloat too much at how his grand plan had played out so well.

It took him a few minutes to figure out where they'd gone to film the next section. He caught Shiloh's eye so she knew his intention of joining the act, and then turned his attention to Vicki.

Shoulders stiff and hands clenched at her sides, she was struggling and far from the relaxed, confident woman she could be. The cameras and attention made what should have been a private moment at home all the more stressful. However, the stiffness did help sell her act as a cold, reserved woman.

It's always been my job to help her release that hot-blooded side.

Jesse came up to her as she unlocked the car. "If you're leaving, take me with you."

"Get lost." Her voice had frosted over, brittle as ice. "Look, kid, I'm trying to protect you."

Ignoring her words, he leaned down and kissed her shoulder boldly, daring a light nip if the jolt of her shoulders was any indication. "I don't need any protection from you, ma'am."

She stared up at him like she didn't recognize him, and Elias had to admit, he was surprised too. He'd never seen this calm, confident side of Jesse before. The heat in his eyes said he wasn't going to stop until he got what he wanted. If he hadn't ever pushed her before, he was about to get a shock of his own.

Vicki's eyes sparked. She shoved him back against the car so hard his breath rushed out. She grabbed his ponytail and jerked his head back, pinning him against the car like a bug, and he melted. His body went pliant, boneless, like she was the only thing holding him up. The only thing still making him breathe. That dependence and ultimate trust was complete and final, a very heavy responsibility.

Vicki saw it too, and she faltered. Before she could stop the scene, Elias stepped up into the shot. She raised her head, her eyes wide and dark with guilt, desire and fear.

Keeping his manner loose, he leaned down so his mouth hovered over hers. "I told you to show me what you want. I meant it."

He kissed her, taking immediate control of her mouth. He smashed her lips beneath his until her teeth dug into that tender flesh. Inhaling her mouth, claiming her breath, he left no doubt in her mind that he wanted her like no one else. Silently, he challenged her. *Fight me. Make me conquer you, while you conquer him.*

When he broke the kiss, she tried to joke, but her voice trembled. "No shock and awe?"

He let out a low, wicked chuckle. "Not unless that's what you want, babe."

Jesse remained motionless against the driver's side door, but his body wasn't soft any longer. In fact, he looked like a gazelle about to leap into flight.

Noting the camera position, Elias shifted slightly so they'd get a good shot of her gown and what he intended to do with it. After all, the clothes were the commercial—not this awkward yet intensely hot threesome they were trying to work out. He pulled on the red bow tied in the small of her back and dragged the red scarf free. "Do you want him?"

Her chin lifted incrementally and her eyebrows rose in challenge. "Yes."

He captured one of Jesse's wrists and looped the scarf around it, then the other wrist so eagerly offered. Elias had no idea what he was doing. Handcuff, yes. Frisk, absolutely. But this bondage shit? Hell no. So he put a big bow in the scarf for show, just like she'd been wearing.

Despite his stick-up-the-ass conservatism, he was starting to think he really could get off on this. "Then I give him to you."

"Blindfold me," Jesse whispered, his voice thick and slow. "Use my shirt. Make me totally helpless."

Elias had never seen anyone so willing to do absolutely anything for another person without a single reservation. *He* didn't give her Jesse—he gave himself wholeheartedly, whether Elias approved or not.

With trembling fingers, she pulled the turquoise cravat loose and wrapped it around Jesse's head. Before she could start thinking about the cameras and what his reaction might be, Elias pushed against her, using his body to trap her against Jesse. While the other man shuddered with bliss beneath her, Elias bit her neck in that tender spot that always made her hot. He held her firmly with his teeth, running his left palm down her flank and hip.

When she began unbuttoning Jesse's shirt, Elias tugged her skirt up. He moved his mouth to her ear, biting her lobe hard enough she jerked against him with surprise.

"I could take you like this while you play with him." He heard the violence rumbling in his voice and he didn't care. Neither did she, by the way she arched and rubbed against him like a cat. "Would you like that? Kissing him while I fuck you? Then maybe when I'm done, you might still have something left for him."

"Hell yeah," she growled out against Jesse's mouth. "Would you like that?"

"God, yes. Do me now."

"Cut," Shiloh called from the sideline.

Biting back a curse, Elias tightened his grip on Vicki and buried his face against her neck. "If I had my service weapon, I think I'd have to shoot her."

She laughed raggedly. Jesse buried his face against her chest. She held him, running her fingers through his hair, but Elias couldn't work himself up to jealousy. Not with her tempting ass tucked against his groin.

"Shiloh, I hope you got enough for the commercial," Vicki said, "because I don't think we'll survive another round."

"At least not in public," Elias whispered against her ear.

She stilled, tilting her head slightly so she could see him out of the corner of her eyes. "Are you serious?"

"Maybe." He blew out his breath in a gruff sigh. "Hell, Vik, you're making me crazy, but I can't seem to make myself care."

"Well, well, well."

Vicki went rigid in his arms. Shit, he'd gotten so caught up in the sensual playing for the commercial that he'd totally forgotten that Mrs. Connagher was going to stop by. So much for cutting the old hag off at the pass.

Ripping off his blindfold, Jesse hopped up off the car like it'd suddenly roasted his ass and joined Elias. Side by side, they turned and faced her with Vicki behind them. She wasn't one to cower or hide...unless the threat was her mother.

The formidable matriarch of the Connagher family wasn't a tall woman physically, nor exceptionally beautiful or stunning by typical beauty standards. She radiated confidence and power, though, and it only took one look in to her dark eyes to see where her children had inherited their steely core. Mr. Connagher had passed away before Elias had the chance to meet him, but he'd have given his right arm to meet the man who'd managed to tame her long enough to sire three children. By Vicki's stories, her parents had truly loved one another.

Mrs. Connagher smiled and chills dripped down Elias's spine. "Here I despaired of you ever settling your mind on one man and now I see two. Does that mean double the grandbabies?"

Chapter Fourteen

Vicki wanted a bottomless pit to open up and swallow her. Her stomach quivered so tight and uneasy that all she wanted to do was whirl away and run off set like demons chased her. What a nightmare. She'd taken great pains over the last few years to make sure Mama only saw her at her best, and they'd still blown up at each other. What the hell would this be like?

Caught panting between Elias and Jesse in risqué clothing. God, please, just kill me now.

Mama hugged Victor and for the time being, took delight in tormenting his fiancée. That gave Vicki enough time to smooth her dress and find her confidence. She'd faced down mean old judges with the power to throw her in jail if he didn't like her blouse. She could certainly deal with Mama.

"Vicki." Mama smiled and held out her arms. Vicki's face felt frozen and brittle, but she hugged Mama and gave her a dutiful peck on the cheek. "How's my girl?"

"Fine, Mama." She knew Mama wanted an introduction or at least an excuse about what was going on, but Vicki refused to give an inch. *Make her ask. That keeps the advantage with me.*

It worked at least a little, because Mama's jaws tightened and her eyes narrowed. She turned to Elias and held out her hand. "Detective Reyes."

"Ma'am."

"I thought you were out of the picture."

His neck turned red, which was almost enough to make Vicki laugh out loud and relax. Almost, but not quite, because she was more worried about the other man standing on her right.

"I'm Jesse Inglemarre, ma'am."

Mama took his hand, squeezing hard evidently, because Vicki noted the way his face tensed a moment before relaxing. His shoulders dropped, his body easing into the fierce grip like he did when she touched him. Suddenly she was so pissed, so mindless with jealousy and fury, that she couldn't breathe. Couldn't move. She wanted to strike out with violence, even against her mother.

"Ah," Mama breathed out and released him. "So the apple doesn't fall far from the tree after all. When you picked Reyes, I honestly started to wonder. I thought maybe I'd been wrong."

"You're never wrong, Mama." Vicki didn't even try to keep the bitterness out of her voice. At least that was better than violence. "I learned that a long time ago. Just another way I've let you down, right?"

"Is that what you think?"

Unperturbed by Mama's unusually quiet voice, Vicki wrapped her arm around Jesse's waist and pulled him against her. With Elias on her other side, she'd be shielded from the fiery darts Mama would lob at her. "I *know* it. First I quit my job at the firm after years of grad school and grueling overtime to try and make partner, all on a lark—to start my own clothing line. Now I'm dating two men at the same time. You've despaired of me ever getting married and settling down."

"Quitting that law firm was the best thing you've ever done."

Braced for an I-told-you-so tirade, it took Vicki several moments to realize that was actually a compliment. Stunned, she could only stare at Mama, searching those dark eyes so like her own for the truth. What she saw horrified her.

A tear streaked down her mother's face. "So that could only be *your* self-doubt, honey, if you think I'm disappointed in you. Same with Reyes. I knew you two were fire and oil, too explosive together. You'd kill each other before you'd ever work out enough of a truce for marriage, but that's exactly what you wanted. In a way, you were punishing me by picking an upstanding man I had to like but you never intended marriage. Don't look at me like that, Beulah Virginia."

Gaping, Vicki flinched at both the use of her real name and the sharper tone of voice, even while Mama dashed her tears away impatiently.

"Don't stand there so innocently shocked. If you'd really wanted Reyes, then you would have demanded he marry you or get the hell out. Forget this polite 'dating' and sometimes sleeping together crap. Either you love him or you don't. Make up your damned mind and quit punishing me."

"I'm not..."

"Aren't you?" Mama cut in, taking a step closer to glare into her face. "You want to play pity party because you think you've let me down, but in reality, I'm the one who let you down, right?"

Vicki backed away but ran into a hard body. At first she thought it was Elias, but he would have protected her from this confrontation. Her brother wouldn't. Victor's hands settled on her shoulders to hold her in place and comfort her at the same time. "Don't run from this conversation, Little V. It's beyond time that you two aired your grievances."

"This is your doing," she whispered, blinking back tears. "You brought her here."

"Yes. Because I love you both and I can't stand seeing you hurt each other any longer."

"You're still mad about something that happened almost fifteen years ago." Mama sighed and dropped her gaze to the floor. Vicki couldn't hold back the tears, then, because her mother looked so dejected. "I let you down and you can't forgive me. Every choice you've made since then was a deliberate act of punishment and rebellion."

Elias pressed closer to her side and whispered in her ear. "What happened?"

She shook her head, but that didn't stop Mama. Nothing would ever stop her. "A smooth-talking devil tried to take advantage of her while she was up north visiting my mother."

The cop in Elias made him tense. Vicki knew he was assuming the worst. "He regretted his mistake pretty quickly when I kneed him in the groin and broke his nose before he could do much but rip my shirt."

Victor laughed. "Then Conn got his hands on the little runt."

"My poor taste in boys nearly got my brother arrested. Strike one for me, right, Mama?" Vicki couldn't keep the sharpness out of her voice, even though her mother winced. "You never trusted me to go up to Miss Belle's alone after that."

Mama's eyes flared with surprise. "That's why you quit going, isn't it? Honey, I had no idea you wanted to go again. We thought you might be scared to go back and deal with the gossip."

She laughed, but the sound hurt her ears. "Right. Have to worry about those gossipers. It was all my fault anyway."

"I never..."

"Yes, you did." Each word rang like a sledgehammer in her head. "You said I should have had better taste than that. You said you were disappointed. *In me.* Not the asshole trying to rip off my shirt. Me."

"Honey, I was out of my mind with worry. As God is my witness, that boy was lucky he had Conn to deal with instead of your daddy. By the time we drove up to Missouri—and knew you were all right—he'd calmed down, but I'd listened to him rant and rave for six hundred miles. Add that to my own rage, and it was all I could do not to horsewhip that fool, no matter how rich and important his family.

"I was not at my best. I apologize. I said the wrong thing. I know it. I never once blamed you for what happened. Never. But you refused to ever let me tell you how sorry I truly am. I love you more than anything in the world, honey. Don't you know that? I'll say it again. I'm sorry. I was wrong to make you feel badly after such a traumatic event."

Vicki had to touch her mouth to make sure she wasn't gaping like a beached fish. She'd never heard her mother apologize or admit that was wrong. Not once in thirty years.

"However," Mama said slowly, drawing the word out.

Vicki groaned out loud. *I should have known an apology was too easy.*

"You had no business dating a boy like that. Yes, his family was rich and influential, but he was all show, no heart. He was like a sleek, flashy horse prancing in the arena, but as soon as you ask him to run a mile, he ends up winded and lame because he's not built to run. You were too concerned with status, fitting in, making the right sort of friends, and that had me worried. I've been worried for a long time, but I couldn't get you to stand in the same room without arguing about something ridiculous."

"I don't care about status."

"The hell you don't. Take a look at that fancy car behind you. Why did you become a defense attorney? Why did you take the job at Wagner & Leeman's in the first place?"

Vicki opened her mouth to retort, but Mama cut her off with a sharp gesture.

"Don't get me wrong. I'm not slamming attorneys. Our justice system needs them. But you didn't help the truly innocent people who need a good defense. You were getting drug dealers and money launderers out of jail when that's exactly where they should have been rotting. It only took meeting your boss one time for me to know he was the worst sort of bottom feeder, every bad cliché and joke about lawyers wrapped up into one. Yet you slaved for him, determined to make partner. And for what? A flashy Jaguar? A high-priced downtown condo?

"And here you are again, pussyfooting around, tied up in knots about your men. Not because they're not willing to work something out for you. Not because you don't love them both, because I can see it as clear as the nose on your face. No, you're afraid of what people will think. You're afraid to follow your heart instead of worrying about climbing some societal ladder that only you care about. You're going to be in the public eye for this fashion show, and you're frozen with indecision because people might talk. There might be *scandal.*"

Vicki didn't know what to say. Her mind felt numb, cold and shaken. Was that true? Did she care too much about what everyone else thought and expected, instead of just following her heart?

"Everybody lets people down no matter how they try not to," Mama said in a dull, heavy voice as she turned to leave. "I'm sorry, Vicki. I let you down. I hope someday you can forgive me."

Bundled up in a quilt—made by Mama—on the couch, Vicki snuggled deeper into Elias's side. He had his arm around her shoulders, while Jesse stretched out on her other side with his head in her lap. She ran her fingers over and over through his hair and tried to think about what Mama had said, but she was hollow inside.

Crying always did that to her.

Elias had managed to come back tonight instead of working late, and her tears had shockingly not driven him off. His fingers made slow, gentle circles on her upper arm. "Why didn't you ever tell me about that jerk?"

"Because." She shrugged, trying to be nonchalant, but Elias let out a low growl. "It's not something I'm very proud of."

"Hell, Vik, you busted the asshole's nose. I'd be pretty damned proud of that."

"I didn't have a crush on him or anything, but I did like the way people treated me when they thought we were dating. Usually my brothers and I showed up for a few weeks and everybody treated us like we had the plague. Once I started dating Jared, everybody wanted to talk to me. I was invited to go to the lake, shopping, everything. A group of us drove up to Springfield and hung out at the mall. That's when I first became interested in clothes and fashion, because I'd never gone to a mall with Mama. She's not a big shopper, and we usually bought all our clothes in town instead of driving down to Dallas."

"When did you decide to become a lawyer?"

A wry smile twisted Vicki's lips. "When my brother was almost thrown in jail for beating Jared up. I'd already broken his nose, but Conn just about killed him. I had to pull him off, and if anyone other than Miss Belle had been there, I'm sure they would have thrown him in prison. It would have been my fault, and I was determined to find a way to get him—and others like him—out of prison. Somewhere along the way, I lost sight of that."

She swallowed hard and forced herself to broach the painful subject they'd been avoiding—but still stewing about—for so long. "When Donnie was killed by one of our clients, I was sick. I mean it, Elias. I threw up in the women's restroom, over and over, on my knees, clinging to the toilet and wishing I'd taken the bullet instead of him. I'd been lying to myself for so long, pretending that I was happy with my job, that I was doing the right thing. When he died, all I could think about was: what if that had been you shot dead? *By my client.* I'll never forgive myself that Donnie's gone, but God, Elias, if it'd been you...I would have killed myself."

"Ah, babe." He held her, pressing his mouth to her temple. "I felt guilty too. I kept thinking that bullet should have had my name on it, not his. I didn't have kids who'd have to grow up without a daddy. I didn't have a wife who'd cry herself to sleep for years. But I finally convinced myself it wasn't my fault. Shit happens, bad shit, I know, but there wasn't anything I could do about it. There wasn't anything you could do about it either. Even dirtbags have rights. I didn't like it, but you were only doing your job."

"I left my office that day and went to the park."

Elias tensed slightly against her. She'd managed to surprise him after all. "Even then, you went to Jesse."

"I was too ashamed to call you. I was afraid you'd curse me out, or worse, just blow me off. God, Elias, if I'd called you and you refused to talk to me, I don't know what I would've done. I was so out of my mind I had to see someone. Someone...safe." She curled her hand around Jesse's cheek and his lips brushed her fingers. "Deep down, I knew he'd be there for me. He wouldn't question or judge me, because I knew Mama was right. Leeman is absolutely a bottom feeder, but when he walks into a courtroom, everyone pales. I guess I wanted people to quiver with fear when I walked into the courtroom too."

"You make me quiver every time I see you. You're one hell of a woman, Vicki Connagher. I'm glad you and your brother beat that punk up. I'm glad you're a strong, powerful woman who's willing to go up against anyone and anything to make sure the law is followed. You were one hell of an attorney, and if I were ever on the wrong side of the law, there's no one else in the world I'd want defending me."

Cupping her cheek, Elias kissed her so tenderly her eyes burned again. Tenderness from him—or her—was as rare as her phone calls to Mama in the last few years.

Jesse sat up, a sheepish look on his face. He scooted away and began to stand up, but she turned and reached for his hand. "Where are you going?"

"It's late. I ought to leave you two alone."

"Not without a kiss goodnight." Elias's voice sounded normal, but when she searched his face, she noted that his jaw was tight. "I might be a mean son of a bitch, but I'm not cruel. We did a lot of tormenting and play today. He's going to need a little more from you than a peck on the cheek."

"Are you sure?"

"I need to see how I'm going to feel when I see you touching him." He ran his hand through his hair and ground his teeth.

"I'll be honest, Vik. It's going to be damned hard for me to watch. But we need to start somewhere."

Jesse slipped off the couch and moved over to kneel in front of her. The sight of him waiting on his knees made her heart thud heavy and hard. Her pulse jumped, her blood hot and sweet, rushing through her veins. The light in his eyes was intoxicating. Touching him, even her fingers stroking his cheeks, increased that feeling of rising desire.

She kissed him, trying to keep it fairly clean for Elias's sake. She didn't want him to see her gobbling up another man, but the way Jesse melted against her made her crazy. Boneless, he sank into her embrace, soft, open and willing for anything she needed. All too quickly, she found herself gripping his bottom lip in her teeth. She dug her fingers into his buttocks, pressing him as close to her as possible.

Breaking the kiss, she dropped her head to his shoulder and concentrated on breathing. Damn it, what had happened to her control? Her desire to protect Elias as much as possible? Another few minutes and she would have shoved her hands down Jesse's jeans.

"Are you okay?" She didn't dare lift her head to seek Elias's reaction. Jesse didn't answer—he knew who she was asking.

"Yeah," Elias replied in a graveled voice that made her shiver. "I've never seen anyone go so limp and eager like that. It's like he's giving you every single thing he's got. His breath. His will. God, no wonder he makes you so hot, Vik. He's begging you to ravish him." He must have leaned close because his hot breath moistened her ear. "Show me some more."

Elias had never thought of himself as a Peeping Tom, but he couldn't deny that he was rock-hard and throbbing at the sight of his woman kissing another man. It wasn't any man, though. If it were anyone but Jesse in her arms, he'd probably be dead. The kid wasn't a threat to him. Vicki wanted him, but she gave Elias no doubts about how much she wanted him too.

She released Jesse's ass to jerk his T-shirt over his head. Using the soft cotton, she tied his hands together in the small of his back. She'd been feeding him well, because he wasn't as painfully thin as when she'd first taken him in. "What do you want?"

"Rough me up a little," he gasped. "Pull my hair or bite me. God, I'd love it if you'd bite me hard enough to bruise."

She wound her fingers in his hair and gave his head an experimental jerk. "Like that?"

"Harder. Force me to bend to your will."

Elias made himself hold his breath for a count of ten and then let it out slowly. Damned if he was going to embarrass himself by hyperventilating...or coming in his pants like a pimply-faced teenager.

She pulled Jesse's head back, forcing him to arch his neck and upper body away from her. She had strong hands, so Elias knew she was pulling hard, giving him what he'd asked for. With her other hand, she began unbuttoning Jesse's jeans. His breathing was loud, rasping through his strained throat.

"Make me wait," he ground out. "Don't let me come without your permission."

"Okay." She twisted her fingers tighter in his hair and pressed her mouth to his neck.

By the way he jerked and groaned, she wasn't kissing him. There was a reason Elias joked that she was like a shark or a crocodile—she'd always loved biting, and the neck and shoulder were her favorite targets. She ran her mouth down Jesse's neck to his shoulder, leaving bites as she went, harder, really working the underlying muscle. He moaned louder, his breath panting, his skin a sheen of sweat.

Finally, she got his jeans unbuttoned. His shoulders bunched, tendons standing out in his neck.

"Not yet." She let out a husky laugh, tracing his ear with her tongue. "You said to make you wait."

"I'm going to die."

"Good," she purred. "Elias loves it when I do this to him."

"The hell I do." He did, though, and she loved it too, because he gave as good as he got. "Why don't you dig those claws into him? He'll really like that."

She cupped Jesse's balls, using her nails to grip that fragile skin. His eyes fluttered shut. Completely surrendered to her, his body hummed and vibrated like a delicate instrument in her hands. It was all Elias could do not to jerk open his own pants. Then she could have a cock in each hand. Maybe even have a contest over who could last the longest when she started using her mouth.

Christ, all the blood must have leaked out of my skull for me to even think about such a thing.

Shifting around to Jesse's side so he was between them, Vicki stared over his shoulder at Elias. Her eyes were dark, gleaming pools of need. She tightened her hands, drawing a louder cry from Jesse. Defenseless, eager, softly pained male, it was a sound that Elias never thought he'd hear, let alone one that would turn him on. But it did. Because the woman he loved had drawn out that sound from the other man's throat.

Still holding his gaze, she bit Jesse's left shoulder, gripping the top muscle in her teeth firmly like a pit bull. He arched in a trembling, straining bow, his cock rising hard and desperate to rub against her, but she only bit him harder. "Please!"

She released him enough to speak. "Say my name."

He shuddered, as though she'd told him to stick his finger in a light socket. "I can't. I'll come, I swear it."

"Then come." She jerked his head to the side and sank her teeth into his straining neck.

"Vicki." Just a whisper that Elias barely heard, but Jesse's body erupted, shaking and twisting in her arms. She held him firmly, unwavering in her strength, and it was so damned moving that Elias couldn't look away.

He could imagine exactly how desperate and wretched Jesse's life must have been on the street. How many times had someone hurt, used and then discarded him? When had anyone cared about his welfare? Had he been able to trust anyone at all to take care of him?

Yet nothing but absolute trust and love gleamed in his eyes when he looked at Vicki. She deserved that trust and that love. Her strength would never falter.

Unlike mine. Shame pierced Elias to the core. He'd abandoned her when she'd needed him the most. He hadn't held her like this when she'd been alone. *I failed her.*

Trembling in the aftermath, Jesse sagged against her. She held him, smoothing her hands over his chest, shoulders, and arms. She kissed the marks she'd left in his throat and whispered something in his ear that made him smile, a slow, heavy-lidded sensual curve of his lips.

Fed by his own guilt, Elias's jealousy suddenly hit the flash point. His stomach churned like he'd eaten nothing but her killer chili for days. Nothing could change his mistakes or roll back the past. If part of his atonement meant he had to share her with another man, then by God he'd swallow his pride and let her have him.

How am I going to keep my sanity when she decides to fuck him for real?

After she jerked the makeshift cotton bindings off his wrists, Jesse pulled up his jeans and stood. He cleared his throat, shifting his feet, and finally muttered, "Good night", in Elias's direction. All he could manage was a curt nod, but that seemed to satisfy the kid.

Unable to meet his gaze, she leaned back against him. He wrapped his arms around her and she whirled around to burrow deep into his embrace. "Sorry. I know that had to be hard."

He didn't say anything, but he couldn't help the involuntary spasm of his arms, clutching her tighter as though he could rip her away from the other man entirely. To reassure her, he kissed the top of her head.

"I know we've talked about the possibilities, but the reality is going to be difficult, embarrassing and emotional. For all of us. I don't want to hurt you, Elias."

"I'm all right, babe." So why did his voice sound like he'd swallowed broken glass? He forced himself to continue without clearing his throat like a hapless fool. "It was actually rather hot. You know I love your passion."

She pulled back enough to look into his eyes. He tried to smile, but it was lopsided and he could only hope agony didn't glint in his eyes like tears. "What can I do to make it up to you?"

"That's easy." He nuzzled her neck, sliding his hand down to knead her ass. "I'm as cheap as a two-dollar whore when it comes to you."

Solemnly, she stood and turned to face him, refusing—or unable—to joke and help him push his emotion away. Holding his gaze, she undressed, not making it a show at all, but a slow, deliberate gift. She looked at him with those dark eyes, so deep and naked with longing for things he didn't know he could give her let alone voice. Had he ever told her that he loved her, really loved her? How could he admit that part of him wanted to murder Jesse, even though he knew that would hurt her?

She slid onto his lap, unbuttoned his shirt and pushed it off, running her hands over him lovingly as she'd done to the kid just a few minutes ago. No matter his turmoil, his erection hadn't faded at all. She took him into her body but it was different. She moved slowly, giving instead of taking, staring endlessly into his eyes, and she was too damned beautiful to bear.

She was tying him in knots and ripping open scabs from wounds he didn't even know he possessed. "What are you doing to me, babe?"

"Loving you." She cupped his face in her hands and pressed soft, gentle kisses over his face. Angel's wings. "What are you doing to me?"

"Loving you." He clutched her, his grip too hard and painful, but he couldn't help it. He found her ear and whispered raggedly, "I do. Always have."

"I know."

Yet shame choked him. She deserved all the words, his heart laid bare. She deserved a ring on her finger, his name, every goddamned thing he possessed. Why did he hold and reserve judgment, protecting himself with that cold, rigid logic that swore she couldn't handle him or his job?

Despite his turmoil, he couldn't hold back his lust. Desire roared through him, consuming him. In seconds, he climaxed, too quickly for her. Shuddering like Jesse had moaned in her arms, he tried to calm his breathing and find his mental faculties again, but all he could do was clutch her. "I don't want to lose you."

"You're not losing me, Elias. Look at me." She pulled his face up and the stern, strong woman who'd marched into courtrooms for battle glared down into his eyes. "You're not losing me. I love you more than ever."

"But I left you. I was out of the picture, as Mama put it so elegantly. I screwed up, babe."

She tucked his face against her breasts and ran those strong, powerful fingers down the back of his skull, kneading his neck gently to help ease the tension vibrating his body. "You're back now. Just don't leave me again."

Chapter Fifteen

The silence in the truck was deafening, but Jesse didn't feel inclined to talk. Trapped in a vehicle with Vicki's other man in rush-hour traffic—it had to be a new circle of hell. *Let him break the ice. See if he has anything nice to say for once.*

"Here's the deal." Elias finally spoke but didn't glance away from the bumper-to-bumper traffic. "Rodgers is a big-mouthed braggart who thinks he has the biggest dick on the squad. He's been giving everybody a bad time, but especially Colby because he's the youngest detective in our division. We're hoping to teach him a lesson tonight that'll convince him to back off before one of us busts his mouth."

"So you're going to let him think he's the greatest card shark in Dallas until he's in deep and then take him for everything but the shirt on his back."

"No." Elias spared a quick glance at Jesse, his mouth quirked with a dark glint in his eyes. "I want his shirt too. This asshole has been riding my partner hard, and Colby's taken everything Rodgers dished without complaint. But enough is enough. That's where you come in."

"You want me to help you play him, get him to bet larger."

"If Colby or I start winning, then he'll know he's being played and he'll jump ship before we can teach him a lesson. He doesn't know you. Nobody on the force knows you. If you play some cat and mouse with him, really get him to playing along and betting heavier, he'll never see it coming."

Jesse turned his head and stared unseeing out the window. "I can do that, sure. Just pretend you don't know me. I'm assuming you can spot me enough cash to lure him into heavier betting?"

"I've got you covered. Besides, it'll be pretty obvious I know you since I'm bringing you to the game. I'll just say you're Vicki's friend."

Friend. That word burned a hole in Jesse's heart.

Elias drove in silence a few minutes. When he started to speak again, he had to clear his throat. "Look, Rodgers is a real ass. I can't vouch for his manners, if you know what I mean."

The cop almost managed to be magnanimous. Jesse grinned at him. "Watch out, Detective Reyes, I might start to think you care about what happens to me."

Elias snorted. "Vicki'll kick my ass if I let anything happen to you."

When they walked up to a dingy, tiny apartment, Jesse had no idea it was Elias's until he used his key to open the door. Inside wasn't much better, just more beige. No pictures on the wall or any color softened the room. The only bright spot was a picture of him with Vicki. Elias was decked out in his dress uniform, and Vicki wore a gorgeous but simple black dress. The smile on her face warmed the room as much it touched Jesse's heart.

"Pretty shitty, I know." Elias tossed his keys on the counter and jerked his head toward the table in the corner where he'd set up the game. "That picture's from the Policeman's Ball two years ago. I didn't go last year."

His last partner's death hung in the silence. For some reason, Jesse felt compelled to say something in her defense.

169

"She cried that day. She kept asking herself over and over what she'd do if that'd been you."

Elias let out a noncommittal grunt, gruff and brash as usual, but Jesse noted the man kept his back to him as he pulled beers out of the fridge.

"If anything ever happened to you, she'd be devastated," Jesse added softly. "But she's proud of what you do."

Elias was saved from having to answer by the doorbell. Colby walked in with another man, but it was clear from their body language that they were far from friends. Rodgers was a meaty, balding man with the reddish nose and cheeks of a hard-core alcoholic. He set those bloodshot eyes on Jesse and guffawed. "I never thought you'd find a more useless excuse for a man than Wade here, but I do believe you've achieved the impossible. Who's this little cream puff?"

"Jesse, meet Detective Frank Rodgers. Frank, this is Jesse Inglemarre, a friend of Vicki's."

Rodgers took a seat directly across from Jesse and helped himself to a beer. "You marry that broad yet? Wait, I know that answer. By the looks of this dump, you haven't."

Colby smiled, just a good-old boy innocent grin that didn't fool Jesse one minute. This man had killed in the line of duty and burned to do it again. "Isn't that why we're not at your place, Frank?"

Rodgers harrumphed beneath his breath. "Are you going to hand over this month's pay to me or what?"

As they started playing, Jesse concentrated on simply watching, quiet and unassuming. Elias and Colby joked about people at work and their various cases, but Rodgers had nothing positive to say whatsoever. For the first three hands, no one even spoke to Jesse. However, he didn't miss the surreptitious looks from Rodgers, slow and reluctant, as though he hated looking but couldn't help himself.

With each look, the man's eyes burned darker with ugly emotion, and Jesse felt himself shrinking moment by moment, hiding, trying to disappear as he'd done on the streets. Lost, dirty, weak, feelings he'd thought he'd left outside of Vicki's home.

Unfortunately, he knew this sort of man all too well.

Rodgers was the kind of man who'd beat the crap of out him...while raping him.

Never again. He closed his eyes and took a deep breath, held it, and then relaxed it slow and easy. He already knew he could survive just about anything, but this time, he had friends. No one was going to hurt him. As Elias had said earlier, Vicki would tear a new hole for anyone who even thought about it. *I don't have to take anyone's shit anymore simply to survive.*

Just thinking about the way her eyes would spark, her body tight and controlled as she stomped over to plow her fist into Rodgers's meaty gut made Jesse smile.

He caught Rodgers's glance again. The man didn't like that smile for all the wrong reasons. So Jesse smiled more. He deliberately made his bottom lip pouty. Thinking about Vicki, he let his eyes smolder. *Just let this asshole try something.*

The more he smiled, the heavier Rodgers bet. And the more he lost.

When Elias's phone rang, he called a pause to the game so he could take the work call in the other room. Jesse took the opportunity to slip into the dark galley kitchen. Breathing rapidly, he rested his head against the fridge and concentrated on deepening each breath. He almost felt high, his brain buzzing, his muscles so loose he didn't know if he could stand for long.

He wanted to laugh. He wanted to call Vicki right now and tell her how afraid he'd been, but how she'd helped him get over it without even being here.

The memory of her scent washed over him, hot and spicy, her hands strong as she held him, her reluctant passion that blasted them both. She made him feel confident, powerful in a way he'd never known before. She gave him the safety to ask for exactly what he wanted and needed, without fear or shame.

How could he ever be afraid again?

A hard hand seized his shoulder and whirled him around. Rodgers loomed over him, trapping him in the dark shadowed corner, his breath sour with beer. "Exactly who are you, boy?"

His life on the streets flashed through his mind. Trapped in a dark alley, hard hands forcing him to his knees, the reek of fear and rotting trash and old whiskey in his nose. The sick pit in his stomach as a stranger jerked open his pants and grabbed his head.

Instead of fear, rage bubbled up inside him. He shoved Rodgers hard enough the man reeled and cracked his head on the cabinet behind him. "Don't touch me!"

Deadly fury twisted Rodgers's face.

Time slowed. Jesse saw the fist coming, but fear didn't cripple him. He ducked enough that the meaty fist only grazed his mouth, while he jerked his knee up into the cop's crotch. It might be a girly move, but nothing disabled a man faster than a hard knee to the family jewels.

Rodgers let out a guttural roar. His face blazed red, his fists ready to pound Jesse into a pulp, but for once in his life, he didn't back down. He even managed to smile at the man despite his sore lip, deliberately emphasizing his dimples. "Come at me again, you son of a bitch, and I'll—"

Suddenly Elias slipped in front of him so fast that one minute Jesse was glaring at the belligerent cop and the next he could only see Elias's broad back. He lunged and Rodgers crashed against the table. Chips clattered to the floor. "What the fuck is going on in here?"

Rage pulsed in Elias so thick and dark he couldn't breathe. He'd neglected to protect an innocent person, let alone a friend, in his own home. Worse, he was the one who'd brought Jesse into harm's way. He'd known exactly what sort of asshole Rodgers could be. Anyone stupid enough to hassle Colby—a former Marine with combat experience—would chew Jesse up and spit him out.

"Hey!" Jesse tugged on his arm, trying to pull him away from the other cop. "I don't need your help."

Elias turned enough to look into Jesse's face and his blood ran cold. "You're hurt. That son of a bitch hit you!" Whirling around, he seized a handful of Rodgers's shirt and jerked him up on his toes, shoving his face down toward the other man's. "How dare you come into my house and put your hands on my guest?"

"The fucking pansy came on to me!"

Jesse surged forward, fists clenched at his sides. Now it was Colby's turn to hold him back. "That's a lie!"

"He was flirting with me! You both saw it, unless you're as blind as a bat."

"So that explains it," Colby drawled.

"What?" Rodgers retorted.

"Why you lost so much." Colby winked at Elias and gave Jesse a friendly slug on the arm. "You were too busy making eyes at our good-looking friend to pay attention to your cards."

Reining his temper back was like holding on to a snarling rabid pit bull with a single strand of thread, but Elias forced out a hard laugh. He eased back on the intimidation factor and released Rodgers. "I can't wait to tell the boys downtown. We finally know Frank's weakness."

Rodgers flushed so dark that his cheeks were a vivid purple. "Not a word, Reyes, or you'll both regret it."

Elias burned to simply snarl and bite a hunk out of the bastard. "Everybody knows you're just driving a desk until you can take your pension. Don't fuck it up by pissing in my territory again, Frank. You leave my friends alone, whether we're on the job or not."

"This little—"

Elias could see the slur forming in the man's eyes. Before he could say it, Elias stepped back into the man's space, chin jutting, fist aching to slam into the man's mouth to shut him for good. "Don't even think about it, Frank."

"I've got pull with the lieutenant. I can get you thrown back on a beat over in Fort Worth with a snap of my fingers."

So much for his plans to keep this away from office politics as much as possible. It was all Elias could do not to drag his fingers through his hair and curse. He shouldn't have put Jesse in harm's way. Then he'd compounded that mistake by losing his temper and putting his hands on Rodgers.

Son of a bitch. I fucked myself into a corner.

"Oh, now, detectives, we don't have to get nasty, do we?" Jesse drawled in a buttery purr that made Elias's eyebrows rise. With a coy little pout, he sidled up to Rodgers and playfully walked his fingers down the man's chest. "You like it rough, huh? How many times has someone noted that you roughed up a witness, just a little? I bet they'll all believe me when I admit that you bloodied my mouth before trying to force me into sucking you off."

Rodgers sagged against the wall. "Never. They'd never believe it."

"He has witnesses." Colby looked over at Elias. "Don't you have a camera handy so we can take a picture of the evidence?"

"You didn't see a thing!"

"It was so dark in that kitchen," Colby replied, his voice going hard and mean. He'd been chomping at the bit to get back at Rodgers for too long. He sure wasn't missing out on his chance now. "I'm not sure what all I saw but it won't look good for you."

Elias could see through Rodgers's bluster. His eyes darted toward the door and sweat poured down his meaty face. If the bastard didn't get his blood pressure calmed down, he'd probably have a coronary before he got home.

All he wants to do is get out of here and forget it ever happened.

"I'll tell you what," Jesse said in an even, calm voice that still echoed with an undercurrent of power. Elias had to do a double take, because he'd never heard the kid talk in such a confident, nearly aggressive way. "You lay off *my* friends, and I'll forget about getting backed into a dark corner in the kitchen. Deal?"

Rodgers straightened and ran a hand over his balding head to smooth back his comb-over. He studiously avoided meeting any of their gazes as he headed for the door and walked out.

"And *I* was never here," Colby said in a dramatic voice, breaking the ice.

Laughing, Elias started to clear off the table. The other two men helped in companionable silence. A new sense of equal footing echoed between them. Jesse had managed to surprise him yet again, confidently dealing with Rodgers's violence and hatred without falling apart. He must have seen a lot of crap like that on the street. Yet he'd managed to clean himself up and had stayed drug free. He'd gotten his life back on track. Yes, Vicki had provided the opportunity, but Jesse was doing the work himself. He'd even managed to help Elias out of the nightmare he'd created by losing his temper.

"Hey, thanks," Jesse said quietly once Colby had moved into the kitchen.

"For what?" *Bringing you here to deal with an asshole and getting your lip busted open?*

"For protecting me. That means a lot to me."

"No sweat," Elias replied in a gruff voice that made Jesse roll his eyes and laugh. Good. The kid was beginning to figure out he wasn't all bite after all.

Colby tossed an ice pack to Jesse. "Yeah, we've got your back, Jesse. But you might want to take care of that lip before you get home, or Vicki'll rip poor Elias limb from limb. I'm out of here." He shook hands with both of them. "I've got a hot date."

Elias groaned. "You're not going out with Mal, are you?"

Colby winked at Jesse. "Maybe."

Elias called after him. "Then you'll be the one ripped limb from limb!"

Surely he was mistaken, because he thought Colby muttered, "God, I hope so."

Chapter Sixteen

The phone would not stop ringing. Harried and stressed with last minute preparations for the fashion show, Vicki finally turned the phone off until she could hire a secretary. The ad had been running on VCONN all week and boy, was it paying off. Shiloh's idea had generated hundreds of orders already.

How am I ever going to keep up? Vicki stared at the stack of forms and despaired. It was a wonderful problem to have, definitely. *More hiring is in my future.*

After this damned show.

She stared at herself in the bathroom mirror, twisting so she could see the sides and back of the gown she'd crafted. Pride brought tears to her eyes. After all these years, she'd finally made something she was proud of. It made her feel beautiful, powerful, invincible, everything she'd need to get through the clamor and glitz tonight. Victor had warned that the media attention would be fierce and the questions might get too personal.

What could she expect after starring in the ad? She could stand there and protest it didn't mean anything, it was just an ad. Or she could smile mysteriously and lead her two men inside.

At least that's what I intend to do. If Elias shows, that is.

He'd promised to escort her to the show, claiming he wanted nothing less than to sit beside her and cheer as her designs came down the runway, but her mind came up with dozens of reasons he'd surely rather absent himself. Not the least of which was his reputation as a Dallas police officer. She understood, which only made her doubt worse. She wouldn't blame him at all for skipping.

She could only pray he wouldn't.

Jesse called from the front room. "Vicki?"

"In here. Come on in."

She checked her makeup one last time and turned back toward the bedroom. With a low whistle of appreciation, he stepped into the bedroom, while she lost her breath as though someone had steamrolled her to the ground. She couldn't tear her gaze away. His eyes commanded her attention, emphasized by the turquoise of his shirt. He'd slicked his hair back in a ponytail, accentuating the lean lines of his cheekbones and his chiseled jaw.

"Wow," she finally managed to say. They'd seen each other in these outfits already, but never alone, without the demands of the set and cameras. This was personal. *Especially with my bed so close.*

He blushed, which only made her want him more. Pulling her gaze away, she turned to dig in the closet for an evening bag that would match the gown better than her normal saddlebag, as Elias sometimes joked. "Are you ready?"

"I need help tying the cravat."

"Ah. Not exactly a common requirement any longer." She tried to chuckle but her throat was too tight. She pulled out a satin clutch that would look nice with her gown, but she lingered in the walk-in closet. So dumb, but part of her was afraid to look too much at him. He was too gorgeous, too tempting for words.

It's just nerves. Her excuse rang falsely in her head.

Gathering her courage, she stepped back into the bedroom but immediately faltered again. Jesse stared at her bed like a starving man.

A tremor sent the gown swishing about her legs. He'd never been this deep into her house. The look on his face made her weak in the knees and so embarrassingly wet she considered going back into the bathroom to change her panties again.

"Which side do you sleep on?"

His voice was deep and low, strumming her spine with desire. She indicated the side closest to the bathroom. "Elias likes to be between me and the door. It's a cop thing."

"Can I..." Jesse was having a hard time breathing too, and when he looked at her, she trembled, scorched by the heat in his eyes. "Smell your pillow?"

Wordlessly, she nodded. She never expected him to stretch out on her side of the bed and bury his whole face where she slept. She took a step closer, opening her mouth to stop him, but it was too late, and she was too close to temptation.

If I touch him while he's in my bed, Elias might come home to a nasty surprise.

Jesse rubbed his face in her pillow, sliding his hands beneath it to lift it up and around him like he was suffocating himself. The memory of him between her thighs, rubbing his face just like that, made her tremble again. Another surge of desire rocked her foundations and she took another involuntary step closer to him. Almost close enough to touch his shoulder. Or to grip that ponytail and yank his head back so she could kiss him.

"You smell so good," he groaned, his voice muffled. He ground his hips into the bed, and she couldn't help but picture him moving between her thighs while she stared up into those stunning eyes. "I could come right now, if you gave me permission."

Too caught up in the image he was weaving for her, she made no answer. He peeked up at her, his lips soft with invitation. "I suppose that would ruin my clothing for the show."

She cleared her throat, but when she spoke, her voice was still ragged. "Definitely. If you sit up, I'll tie your cravat."

Control yourself, Vik. She watched him sit on the edge of the bed, tilting his head back as she neared. *You can do this without losing your mind.*

She tied the cloth around his neck, even while her mind conjured images of her tying his hands behind his back, or wrapping the silk around his cock and tying it in a huge bow. *So I can untie it with my teeth.*

Groaning out loud, she pushed that image away and changed the subject to the one most likely to keep her hands— and mouth—to herself. "Is Elias here yet?"

Jesse's eyes narrowed and he searched her face. Evidently she wasn't so good at hiding her doubts after all. "No."

This kind of event certainly wasn't Elias's favorite thing to do. If he wasn't there, the questions might be less, because people wouldn't recognize him. But if she showed up with two men on her arm, after there had been two men in the commercial—one of which was easily identified since Jesse hadn't worn any mask—then the gossip would spread like wildfire.

Here I go again, worrying about what everyone else will think. She scowled at herself, which made Jesse arch his brows

180

with surprise. She forced a laugh and let her hands settle on his shoulders. Much safer than playing and tugging on that tempting ponytail. "Sorry, I'm hearing Mama's voice in my head. Either way, we'll be fine."

"Do you think he'll make it?"

She hesitated. There could be a million and one very justifiable reasons Elias might be delayed. If he got a big break in a case, or there was an accident on the freeway, or a murder in his district...

"I made it."

They both jumped at his voice, guiltily, like he'd caught them doing more than talking about him. Leaning against the doorjamb, he gave her a sardonic wink. He'd already dressed for the evening. Dark to Jesse's light, hard to soft, grim to demanding to light and giving, he, too, managed to take her breath away.

He lifted his chin and pointed at the neck cloth of the black silk. "Did I tie it fancy enough?"

She walked over and ran her hands over his chest, checking the fit, she told herself, but she already knew it fit him perfectly. She hadn't had time to make him an entire suit—and he wasn't in the fashion show—so he'd paired her shirt with a black pin-striped suit. The thin silver stripes in the coat helped relieve the unrelenting black, but the color definitely suited him. "You look great. Are you sure you want to come tonight?"

"Wouldn't miss it, babe." He kissed her, but she sensed him watching Jesse over her shoulder. Always the cop, he was carefully cataloguing the other man's reaction, and of course, reaffirming his claim on her in this room. His mouth wasn't demanding or hard, so she couldn't tell if he was jealous or not to see Jesse here with her, no matter how innocently. "I just hope the job cooperates long enough for me to stay the entire night."

"It's the thought that counts. Making the appearance with me." Her lips wobbled, so she simply skipped ahead to, "Thank you."

Watching Vicki come into her own made Elias so proud that his chest ached. Cameras flashed in all directions. A glitzy crowd clamored and pressed closer, sending his blood pressure rising higher. This kind of event was a cop's nightmare. He scanned the crushing crowd constantly, watching for anyone acting strangely, who seemed fixated on Vicki or any of the other guests.

He gripped her elbow and kept her close, but she didn't seem to mind. In fact, every time she turned her face up to him she beamed. Her eyes glowed like starbursts had exploded in those dark depths and her cheeks were flushed.

She's never looked more beautiful.

He had a sudden vision of her walking down a church aisle toward him. Would she glow as much? Could she possibly look more beautiful in a white wedding dress? *Only if you have the balls to ask her.*

Surely part of that warm glow was due to the handsome young man on her other arm. Jesse cleaned up real good, too good, Elias admitted. The kid looked like a cover model for a fashion magazine. Women's heads were turning left and right as Jesse walked by, but he had eyes only for Vicki. Hell, Elias couldn't even blame him, because he was having a hard time looking anywhere but her direction too. This was her night, a dream come true. So by God, he was going to smile until his face broke, clap until his hands hurt, and cheer until he lost his voice as her designs came down the runway.

And then his phone buzzed.

Cursing silently, he pulled the phone out of his inside jacket pocket. Shit. He met her gaze and that glorious smile faltered. It damned near broke his heart.

Ducking his head, he backed away a few steps to answer the call. "Somebody'd better be dead."

"Several, in fact," Colby replied. "Looks like we're on the verge of a cartel war."

Elias sighed, but he couldn't bring himself to look at her yet. He couldn't bear to see the disappointment on her face. *Someday, she's going to hate me. That's why I should have done the noble thing and left her to enjoy Jesse.*

Wincing, he rubbed his chest absently. "Pick me up—"

"Already outside," Colby broke in. "I gave you as long as possible."

"Thanks, man. I'll be out in a few."

Elias stared down at the phone, trying to think of an easy way to break the news. Either she'd be pissed as hell or so hurt she might cry, and if the latter, then he was going to ask his partner to shoot him. If she were only pissed, then he'd have to remember to order flowers. Lots of flowers. And he'd better be nicer to the kid.

Hell, who was he kidding? He'd already bent over backward for them. He'd watched them together and not committed murder. It was a start, right?

Grow some stones, he growled at himself. Whirling around, he put on his best badass cop face, but immediately felt that mask slip off because Vicki stood just a foot away. By the resignation in her eyes, she knew he was leaving. Guilt tightened around his throat like a noose, but at least she wasn't crying, thank God.

"We've got trouble. I've got to go."

Smoothing the lapels of his jacket, she gave him a tiny nod. "I know. Do what you do best, Detective Reyes."

"Babe…"

She smiled and he could only picture her as a kid giving a brave little smile to her rough and tumble older brothers. "It's okay, Elias. I know you have to go and I understand. It means the world to me that you came tonight."

Still, he hesitated. He felt like crap for leaving, like it was his last, only chance to prove how much he cared for her. Jesse wasn't leaving her big event. A dozen drug dealers wouldn't be able to pry the former druggie away from her side.

"I'm not mad." She gave him a firmer tug on his lapels, her eyes sparking with that familiar Vicki flare he loved so much. "Disappointed, yes. Pissed, no. I understand. Go. Save people. And remember—" she leaned up on her tip-toes and brushed her mouth against his, "—that I love you."

It was surreal to walk down a runway. Just a few weeks ago, Jesse had been walking down the street with every precious scrap of possessions he owned on his back. Now he wore brand-new clothes he had no hope of ever affording, cameras flashed, and people applauded. None of it was real except the light in Vicki's eyes.

God, she was so gorgeous. She glowed with happiness. Her designs were on his back, so it was easy to saunter with pride down the runway. She made him forget the hopelessness and years of hunger and suffering. She made him forget everything.

Afterward, they stood together drinking champagne that probably cost more than a year at his cheap shack of an apartment. Countless people came up to them, smiling, shaking hands, like he was somebody. They looked him in the eye instead of ducking their heads and quickening their steps, hoping he wouldn't beg.

"Is this who I think it is?"

At the woman's snotty voice, he stiffened. All the shame and desperation of a life on the streets came roaring back. Filth, stench, shame, he'd never be able to wash it off, no matter how many showers Vicki let him take.

"Yes, it is." She tightened her grip on his arm and leaned against him. Her touch gave him the courage to lift his head and meet the other woman's incredulous stare. "Susan, this is Jesse. Jesse, this is Susan Tolbert. Are you still an attorney for Leeman & Wagner?"

"Yes, partner now." The woman looked Jesse up and down, as though she just couldn't believe her eyes. "This is your artist we teased you about?"

"He sure is." Vicki looked up at him and smiled. It was like a cloudy sky suddenly opened up and a powerful bolt of pure sunshine beamed down on him, washing away all those bad days on the streets. "And he's mine, all mine. I always knew he was special."

It was all he could do not to fall at her feet and throw his arms around her legs.

Take me now. Please, please, make me yours.

On the way back to her home, he kept a firm grip on his emotions. She'd claimed him in public, even to her old friends. She'd claimed him on television with Elias at her back. The only thing that remained was her bed.

He couldn't stand the wait, the agony, the endless need, but he had no choice. In truth, he wouldn't have it any other way, but that sure as hell didn't make the need any less. She'd given him everything. The least he could do was wait until she was ready.

Silently, he resolved over and over not to say a word tonight. Yes, Elias had left and would probably not come home tonight. It'd be the perfect time for Jesse to put a move on her and hope she would take him all the way this time. But he couldn't do that to her.

He walked her upstairs but stood in the door without entering her apartment. She talked nonstop, giddy over how much her design she'd donated had gone for at auction and how much buzz the commercials had generated. Jesse just watched, drinking in her joy and energy, while every muscle ached.

She finally noticed that he still stood in the door. "Come in, silly. Let's celebrate. Do you want a beer? A glass of wine?"

Whatever weak determination she might have seen on his face was lost as soon as she took his hand. He followed her inside like a lamb to slaughter. "Whatever you're having would be great."

She laughed softly and stepped closer, inviting his arms to come around her while her own wound around his neck. She dropped her head against his shoulder and his heart skipped, stumbling along to a rapid thunder of hope and dread, both. So close. If she turned him away again...

"I already had two glasses of champagne at the party. I don't want any more alcohol."

"Okay," he murmured, trying not to let his voice thrum with need.

"I just want..." Slowly, she lifted her head and gazed into his eyes. "You."

Every muscle in his body went ramrod straight. He shook with tension. Surely he hadn't heard her correctly. "Are you drunk?"

Laughter spluttered out of her and she tightened her arms around his neck. "No. Just ridiculously happy. I'm tired of being miserable and doubting myself, Jesse. I know what I want, and that's you, tonight, in my bed."

"Elias—"

She arched a brow at him as if to say, *Do you honestly want to talk about him right now?* "He knows, Jesse. I'll deal with the fallout. I've been nothing but honest with you both. I waited to be sure, and I know. I know in my heart that I need you. I need you now, tonight, every night. My only question is what do you need?"

"You," he replied immediately, swallowing back the tumbling words of desperation and hope and love tearing his stomach apart. "Whatever you want."

"No. This isn't about me. This is about you. The only thing I need is to know exactly what *you* need tonight."

He closed his eyes, trying to hold back the emotion and desperation tearing him up. She'd be horrified if she saw that ragged, dark need in his eyes, an endless black hole that could never be satisfied. Not for long, he feared. She might take the edge off, but he'd always need more, need her to go further, take him harder, longer.

I can't ask for too much—she might send me away. I'll die if she sends me away.

"Jesse," she whispered, stroking his cheeks with her fingers. Her breath fluttered on his throat. Her body heat radiated against him, solid and warm after the coldness of the

187

street. But it was the light in her eyes that drew his heart toward her. "Don't be afraid to tell me what you need."

His eyes burned with hot guilt and shame. He trembled but couldn't utter a word. This gentle side of hers moved him as much as the commanding, confident side. Perhaps more, because it was so precious and rare.

"I can take it. Whatever you want, I promise I won't let you down. I'll see that you get it. Don't you trust me?"

"I do." He panted, trying to hold back the fierce surge of need threatening to bare his soul. "I trust you. I love you, Vicki."

"Then trust me to take care of you." She cupped his face in both hands firmly, digging her fingers into his cheeks to make sure he met her gaze. "Tell me what you need most of all. When you lie downstairs in your bed and think about me, what do you want me to do? Do you want me to tie you up?"

"No, not really. It's fine if you want—"

She squeezed harder, a warning. "Do you need me to hurt you? I don't have any equipment. I can call Mal if there's something specific you think we need."

"No! God, no, don't, please. I just..." He took a deep breath and squeezed his eyes shut so he wouldn't have to see her reaction. "Fuck me, use me, take me over and over whether I want it or not. I do, I promise, but I don't want to have a choice. Make me raw, make me groan and beg, make me plead for you to stop even when I don't want you to. Make me climax so hard I pass out. I don't care. Just fuck me. Please."

Trembling, he waited, dreading every moment of silence and hating himself for his cowardice. He should have kept his eyes open. He should have seen the fleeting emotions in her eyes so he'd be prepared, instead of standing here dumb and blind. *I'd know if I should leave tonight or sneak away tomorrow morning.*

She gripped his ponytail hard, jerking him slightly up on his toes. Hair pulled, bringing tears to his eyes, and she yanked the holder out. "When you're in my bed, I want your hair loose and you naked."

His ears roared and he swayed slightly, settling back down on his heels. Words, questions tumbled in his head and he finally pried his eyes open. She smiled, a hard, cold, smile of gleaming teeth that made the hair crawl at the base of his neck even while his erection surged against his pants.

"Get busy."

He jerked his pants open and his fingers flew over the buttons of his shirt. "Yes, ma'am."

Chapter Seventeen

She tried to wait until he was actually in her bed. The sight of his gorgeous ass hurrying before her toward her bedroom, compounded by the fire in his eyes every time he looked back over his shoulder at her, made her tight and swollen with need. She'd been denying them so long, too long, ridiculously afraid, and of what? Wanting him too much? Loving him too much?

He had to pause his headlong rush toward her bedroom to bend down and work his shoe out of the jumbled material of his pants. As soon as he straightened, she slammed him against the bedroom wall just as Elias had done to him that first night. Jesse went eagerly, even though he outweighed her. He could have pushed her off or told her to stop, but she knew he wouldn't. That was his appeal...and his danger.

He'll never tell me to stop.

He wanted to be taken however she wanted without her stopping to get his consent. That's what he wanted most of all. The weight of responsibility settled around her heart so thickly that she couldn't breathe. He'd never tell her no, even if she was hurting him. In fact, he wanted to be hurt, if she was the one doing it.

Sensing her hesitation, he whispered, "I know you won't really hurt me."

She pressed her face against his back and tightened her arms around him. "I hope so."

"If I'm ever really scared, I'll tell you."

Would he? He said he wanted to beg. He wanted her to use him coldly and selfishly to please herself.

"How about I call you 'Beulah Virginia' when I need you to stop?"

She couldn't help the startled snort that escaped her. "Yeah, that would work. I'll jump up and look around for Mama."

"Your mama scares the shit out of me."

Her throat tightened, but she refused to let that old regret and pain tarnish this moment with Jesse. "Yeah, me too."

"Mal scares the shit out of me too. But you don't, Vicki."

An odd sort of peace flowed over her, as though someone had wrapped her up in a warm, cozy blanket and tucked her into bed with a fairytale. He wanted her to do her worst to him, yet he wasn't afraid of her. Blinking suddenly hot eyes, she wrapped her hand around his cock and nuzzled his neck. "Let's see what we can do about that, then."

She licked and bit his neck until he sagged against the wall. His breathing was loud in the silence between them. The harder she bit him, the more he slipped and shivered against her. She went to her knees and gripped his ass cheeks, squeezing and kneading. His thighs trembled and he groaned at the feel of her breath against his skin. The hard, rounded muscle filled her hands and refused to yield to her teeth, giving her a nice mouthful to grip and torment.

"Vicki, please!"

She released the bite and leaned back to trace the indentation of her teeth with her fingers. "Maybe you want to roll over then."

He did, immediately, which shocked the hell out of her despite everything she'd learned and done with him already. She'd never known a man who'd offer his private bits to a bite-hungry woman, even if she was on her knees. Elias would only let her have her way with him once they'd both burned off some of the fire.

Jesse pressed his back against the wall and widened his stance like he'd need to brace himself for whatever she'd do, but by God, he was going to take it. And enjoy it. Even if it killed him.

Holding her breath, she leaned in close and brushed her cheek against the satin steel of his erection. He let out a shaking sigh and instinctively rocked his hips toward her. She gripped his thighs above his knees, his muscles trembling. Such a turn on. Yet she lingered, making herself wait. She rubbed her hair against him and brushed her mouth against his inner thigh, but she didn't bite.

His breathing grew louder, more labored, his thighs shaking beneath her hands. He could have gripped her head and thrust himself deep into her mouth, but he didn't. Not Jesse. It wasn't in him to take what he wanted.

He wanted to be *taken.*

She turned her head and snagged his cock in her mouth lengthwise. Gripping him in her teeth firmly, she let a low growl rumble her lips and gave him a little shake like a dog with a bone in its mouth. Releasing him, she looked up at his face. His mouth hung open, sweat streaked his cheeks, and his eyes were closed, but his entire body was loose and relaxed against the wall, barely holding his weight upright.

So beautiful. It hurt her heart to look at him, so open, willing and honest, ready to do whatever she asked. She'd never felt this out of control and yet solemn at the same time. He hadn't touched her, but she was hot and slick, more than ready to feel him thrusting deep. Her nipples were so hard her breasts ached.

The thought of his mouth on her made her shudder. She'd explode.

She licked just the tip and he jolted, his eyes flying open to latch onto hers. "Whose cock is this?"

"Yours," he replied without hesitation.

She stood, fighting back her own desire. She wanted to drag him down to the floor and ride him until he screamed. Turning away, she closed her eyes and took a deep breath. Another. They'd never have another first time together. She wanted to make it last as long as possible, to give him everything she could possibly give. After the way he'd nearly come just from smelling her pillow, he deserved better than the floor.

Still, it felt so strange to leave him standing against the wall. She'd put him there and hadn't told him to follow or join her, so he waited. His entire body seemed tuned to her, listening with more than his ears, waiting, hoping, praying for her next command.

Jumpy and needy, her skin felt like it was going to crawl off her body. Making herself wait, though, seemed to help calm the ravenous beast down a little. She slipped out of the dress and carefully draped it over a chair. It'd wait a few hours to hang properly.

At the edge of her bed, she turned to face him and slowly removed her panties and hose. She'd gone all out and picked up some lace-edged thigh-highs. When she'd ordered them online, she'd pictured tormenting Elias, but the heat in Jesse's eyes made her glad. Glad that she'd bought them, glad that he was here. She missed Elias and she didn't want to lose him again, but Jesse deserved a night with her full, undivided attention. What they worked out long term would include both men. *I hope.*

Scooting back on the mattress, she fluffed up her pillow and reclined back against the headboard. Still braced against the wall, Jesse looked like he was ready to pounce, instead of melting into a steaming puddle on the floor. Letting a smile curve her lips, she trailed her fingers over her belly, watching him. His eyes flared and he licked his lips, but he didn't leave his spot.

"Is there something here you want?"

He gave her a jerky nod.

"Something's missing." She trailed her fingers lower, teasing herself as much as him. God, she was sopping wet. "I need something right here." She let her head tilt back and opened her legs wider, giving him a good view. "I need you."

Before she could draw another breath, he was there, sliding up between her thighs, his mouth finding her fingers. He sucked them into his mouth and groaned, stroking with his tongue until she pulled her hand away and threaded her fingers in his hair. Watching his face, she tightened her grip until his eyelids fluttered. His pulse beat frantically in the side of his neck and his breath panted against her heated skin.

"I'm going to show you exactly where I want you." She gave a firm tug, drawing another groan from his lips. "Nothing but your mouth can touch me right now. Understand?"

"Yes, ma'am."

With a twist of her wrist, she jerked his head to the side. "Vicki."

194

He shuddered. "Vicki, yes, please."

When she'd first brought him here, she'd envisioned the slow, torturous glide of his tongue, but now, it was too late. Too much playing for them both, too much waiting, too much needing. Without another word, she dragged his head down and lifted her hips, grinding against his mouth, his chin, using the stubble on his cheeks to send herself spiraling. He still managed to sink his tongue into her and she cried out, pressing him harder against her.

The climax rocked through her, winding muscles tighter until her bones ached, her toes curled, and her heart thudded so hard she could hear the thunder of her pulse echoing in her head. Endless pleasure coursed through her, sending her higher, longer, until she couldn't stand it. She tried to pull his mouth away, but he resisted, digging his tongue deeper into her until she screamed his name. Only then did he rise up and gasp for air. "That's what I needed to hear."

She dragged him up her body, wrapping her arms and legs around him. He slid inside effortlessly, without fumbling or hesitation, and she locked him against her heart. He simply lay against her, his only movement the slight shifting as he breathed and the tremor in his shoulders. Only when she felt the dampness on her cheeks did she realize he was crying.

"Jesse?" Horrified, she cupped his cheeks, lifting his face so she could search his eyes. "Are you okay? Did I do something wrong?"

"I'm home," he whispered, and the smile he gave her turned her heart inside out. "I've never had a home until you."

"I don't want you to leave. Ever."

He smiled again, boyish and sweet but also sensual. The heat blazing in his eyes had nothing of innocence. "Is that an order, ma'am?"

"Yes." She pulled him down so she could brush her mouth over his lips, nibbling softly. "And my next order..." She hesitated, loving the way his eyes sparked. His muscles tensed, ready and willing to do whatever she told him. She'd never known such power, nor felt such tenderness welling in her heart. "Make love to me."

He braced his elbows on either side of her and shifted his weight. Not exactly a thrust, but he moved inside her, stroking ever so slightly, but it was enough to make her moan. He moved again, his mouth caressing hers. When he cried out her name, this time she was the one crying.

After seeing a body—in tonight's case, three victims—lying in the street, Elias always thought about Donnie, his partner in justice for almost ten years. He'd always envied Donnie's family. When the cases were horrible and the violence and antipathy bore down too hard, Donnie had gone home to his wife. She'd always known when he'd had an especially bad night. Without saying a word, she'd simply wrapped her arms around him and held him tight.

Elias had imagined she'd guided her husband up to their bed and they'd simply lain there in the night, holding each other. In the months since he'd broken up with Vicki, he'd ached to come home to her and wrap her up in his arms. God, he'd ached to just hold her and feel her hold him back. To know that someone outside of the police force cared whether he came home or not.

He wasn't surprised to find her apartment silent when he unlocked her door at six o'clock in the morning. She'd never been a morning person, and he figured she hadn't gotten home until late after the gala anyway. At that thought, he winced.

He'd meant to pick up some flowers or something to make up for having to leave before her show, but he'd totally forgotten. All he'd wanted to do was come home, slip into bed beside her...

Frozen, he stared at the rumpled sheets. Her bare thigh entwined with two muscular legs. Her hand cupped a buttock, holding another man close.

Another man. Jesse. She'd done it.

Dizzy, Elias listed to the side and half fell against the doorjamb. He propped himself up and tried to think. To calm down the predator side of him rearing up and showing those ugly teeth. He'd known this day would come. She'd warned him. He'd warned himself every time he saw the way she looked at the kid. Yet he couldn't help but wonder if she'd decided to punish him for leaving early last night. It made perfect sense in a cold-hearted, vengeful sort of way. He'd bailed on her once again, and to pay him back, she'd come home and dragged her cabana boy into her bed.

Rage bubbled and sizzled in his mind, eating away at his control like acid. His right hand automatically reached for his weapon on his hip, like he'd just pulled over a known drug lord for speeding. His fingers itched to pull the trigger. On her. On Jesse. Hell, on himself. Thank God he'd already locked his gun in the safe from habit.

Payback's a bitch.

His hand hurt, forcing him to shake out the fist aching to pound that handsome young face into a bloody pulp. He must have made a noise or maybe it was just her sense of self-preservation that woke her up. Sleepy-eyed, hair tousled, she looked so damned gorgeous he wanted to slam her flat on her back and fuck her senseless, even though she'd taken another man into her bed.

"Elias," she whispered.

Her eyes went wide. She carefully untangled her limbs from the greedy little bastard lying beside her. Damned idiot should have been dead already. How had he'd ever survived the streets by sleeping through the worst few seconds of danger he could have ever faced?

A snarl twisted Elias's face.

Hers crumpled. She looked like someone had just torn one of her beloved brothers limb from limb.

"How dare you look at me like that," he retorted in a low, mean voice that he hated. God, he hated sounding like his mean father who'd thought nothing of beating his family into submission. "You're the one fucking another man."

"Not *any* man. Only Jesse. You know—"

The kid shot upright and grabbed at the blankets like some shy little virgin.

"Only Jesse," he mocked. "Only the homeless druggie. Only a kid five years younger than you who's fucked more men than women in the last ten years of his life. Is that what you want, Vik? You want to see me with a guy?"

"Shut up! Don't you dare say things like that about him!"

She took a defensive position between him and the bed, like she'd take him down to protect Jesse. *Again, she's choosing him over me.*

"He's mine." Tears pooled in her eyes, but she didn't back down. She didn't even reach out to him, like she knew he'd probably snap and bite like a rabid dog. "I love you, Elias, but I won't let you hurt him. I love him too and he's mine to protect now, even from you."

"Damn it, don't you dare cry." Whirling, he tore through her house toward the front door. "Don't stand there and expect me to pretend like I didn't come home and find you in bed with another man. I'm not a fool, Vik. Hate me for leaving you last night, fine, but don't punish me with another man."

"Elias, just listen for a minute." He paused in the door but didn't turn around. He couldn't bear to see the hurt and desperation in her eyes. "For what it's worth, I didn't sleep with him last night to punish you. It was just...time. I wanted him, not to punish you, but to love him. I've never lied to you about how I felt about him."

"So you took him. I got it. I understand perfectly."

"I still love you more than ever."

He couldn't help the derisive snort that escaped his mouth. "Yeah, babe, somehow I have a hard time believing that."

The door slammed in her face. Elias was gone. Vicki stared after him, replaying his parting words over and over in her mind. The look on his face. Such rage, hatred, disgust. He looked at her like she was the most revolting excuse for human skin he'd ever seen in his life. How could he look at her like that after everything they'd been through?

They'd talked about this so many times. It'd been incredibly hot to call him up and whisper all the naughty things she'd done with Jesse. She'd never hidden anything from Elias, but the reality had been too much for him to deal with.

Behind her, the rustle of sheets told her Jesse had gotten up. She brushed the tears away and turned to face him. He stood beside the bed, tugging on his pants. His hair hung down in his eyes and his shoulders were slumped and small, like he was trying to make himself appear harmless and defenseless against the big bad cop.

"So you're leaving me too?"

He straightened a bit and shook his head enough to get the hair out of his eyes. Even now the bright color of his eyes pierced her to the bone. Another flood of tears trickled down her cheeks. "I'm sorry, Vicki. I never meant for this to happen."

"I know. Me neither."

He hesitated, watching her like he might have to make a run for safety, one leg in his pants and the other still bare. He looked lost, already assuming that invisible persona of the streets, trying to blend in and hide.

She choked back a sob and swiped the tears off her cheeks with both hands. "You said I was your home."

Finally, he was there, wrapping her tight against him. She sobbed into his chest while he murmured in her ear and rocked her gently back and forth. Just like that day in the park when she'd found out that Donnie was dead.

Now I've lost Elias too.

"Do you regret taking me last night?"

She breathed in Jesse's sweet coconut scent. "No, never. I'm glad, Jesse, even if you decide to follow him out the door."

"It might be for the best."

She raised her head and searched his eyes, clutching him tighter. "Absolutely not. I've never been happier than these past weeks with you. You've helped my dreams come true. Those dreams will die without you."

"It was never my intention to come between you and Elias."

"I know, and I love you for it. Please don't leave unless that's really what you want."

"That's the last thing I want, Vicki." He dropped his forehead against hers and wrapped his body around hers. More than a hug—he used his whole body and being to hold her. "I can't breathe at the thought of leaving you. But if you ask me to leave, I will."

She tightened her arms around his neck and hopped up to wrap her legs around his waist. He gathered her closer, shifting her higher in his arms. "Come to bed and hold me."

Cuddled in his arms, she tried to relax. She tried to remember all the wonderful things that had happened to her in the past twenty-four hours. Her line had been a success. Her donation had sold for an incredible amount of money to benefit charity. She had an attentive, sexy lover in her bed.

Yet she couldn't forget that her back was cold and Elias's spot between her and the door was empty.

Chapter Eighteen

Cradling the phone with her shoulder, Vicki stirred chopped chocolate into the brownie batter. She'd probably gain ten pounds waiting and hoping that Elias would come back. The phone rang and rang until finally rolling to his voicemail. Dread choked her but she didn't cry any more. She'd run out of tears while Jesse held her.

Even at his worst just after his partner had been killed, Elias had always answered her calls. Yeah, he'd been short with her. A few times he'd refused to talk to her, using the job as an excuse, but he'd always at least answered. Now he wouldn't even take her calls.

Her fingers trembled but she dialed another number. She didn't think about it for fear she'd just hang up. As soon as she heard the click she didn't wait for anyone to speak. "Mama?"

"Vicki, honey, what's wrong?"

Okay, so maybe she wasn't out of tears after all. She swallowed hard, trying not to blubber like a little kid. She'd lost countless boyfriends over the years and she would've rather cut off her arm than discuss it with her mother, but Elias was different. Losing him made her feel like someone had cut out her heart.

"Are you hurt?" Mama's voice sharpened, but she wasn't one for hysterics. "Where are you?"

"Elias left." Vicki finally made her voice work. "He came home and found me with Jesse."

Several moments of silence made her stomach tighten. What had she been thinking to call Mama of all people? She'd probably been rehearsing a lecture since last week when she'd seen Vicki with both men. Hell, she'd been telling her "I told you so" for years.

"Oh, honey, I'm so sorry. After what I saw the other day, I thought you had an understanding with him."

Relief made her shoulders droop but unfortunately cranked up the waterworks even more. "So did I. He knew everything, Mama. I never lied or hid from him. But he came home and saw me...."

"And he walked out."

"Yeah. Now he won't return my calls."

Mama sighed. "Come home, honey. We'll make your favorite brownies. You can bring the young man too. I know you won't want to leave him behind."

Closing her burning eyes, Vicki couldn't breathe for a minute. It meant the world to hear the acceptance in her mother's voice. Yeah, she wouldn't want to leave Jesse behind, even if that meant she lost Elias forever. Mama got that without even hearing the details of Jesse's life before he came to her. "I've got a batch of brownies already started."

"Somehow I already knew that. It's a good thing you didn't take after your grandma. She would've poisoned your cop."

She managed to smile and even laugh a little. "Yeah, Miss Belle could make a batch of brownies and wipe out the entire Dallas police force." *My cop.* Her throat and head ached, and all she wanted to do was crawl back into bed. The business line had been ringing off the hook all day. This should have been one of the highest days of victory in her entire life. Her line had been a success. People were calling to place orders.

And all she wanted to do was drive home and let her mama spoil her with brownies.

"Give him time, honey," Mama said in a gentle voice she'd only rarely ever heard. "No alpha wolf is going to welcome another male pissing in his territory, let alone sniffing around his mate. His pride is stinging. Give him enough time to let the pain in his heart override his hurt pride and he'll come home. Who knows, if you play him right, you might even get him to grovel."

Vicki shook her head. "Elias doesn't grovel."

"Oh, I imagine you and your young man might be able to come up with something that will make even your cop come begging."

Her face burned like she'd just stuck her whole head in the hot oven. "Um, thanks, Mama. Really, I mean it. I was afraid you'd lecture me or tell me good riddance or something."

"Just promise me one thing, honey. When your cop slinks back home and grovels enough to win an Academy Award, I want to see a ring on your finger the next time you come home to the ranch."

"A ring? Oh, Mama, I don't know..."

"Honey, any man who loves you enough to share you despite his pride is worth marrying and keeping forever."

"I don't think he wants to get married again. He had a rough time with his first wife. She hated that he was a cop and was constantly trying to get him to quit and find a safer job." *Besides, I don't know that he loves me enough. He's not here, is he?*

"Do you want him to quit the force?"

"No."

"Then marry him."

"But..."

"I didn't raise a doormat, Beulah Virginia." Vicki winced at her Mama's raised voice and held the phone away from her ear. "If you want this man, you tell him to marry you or get the hell out. I love you. Come home as soon as you can."

"I love you too, Mama."

Jesse came to the doorway. The paleness of his face rocked her off her feet, the world crumbling beneath her into an abyss. "Something's up—I've got to go."

"Call me, honey."

"I will. Bye." She went to Jesse and he took both her hands in his even though she still held the phone. "What's wrong?"

"Did you ever reach Elias?"

She shook her head. Her heart pounded, her head so light it was going to float away like a balloon. Her knees trembled. "What's wrong? What happened?"

"I just heard the news. A cop..." Jesse hesitated and he gripped her hands so hard the plastic casing on the phone popped. "They were clearing out a known drug house and a cop was shot. He...died."

"Oh dear Jesus." She jerked her hands free and dialed Elias's number again. Her fingers were so cold and numb that she got it wrong and had to cancel the call, cursing the whole time. "Damn it, Elias, you'd better answer the phone. Answer it, damn it!"

Tears blurred her vision. His voicemail. Again. She squeezed the phone, fighting back the hysterics. Sobbing and wailing wouldn't help anyone, least of all Elias. *He's not dead. He's fine. He's just pissed off at me.*

But he'd never let her calls roll to voicemail like this.

Biting her lip so hard she tasted blood, she raced over to the fridge and found his partner's number. The phone rang twice, three times, and she was crying, her shoulders shaking. She nearly sank to the floor, but Jesse was there, holding her, keeping her on her feet. Dear God, Elias. He couldn't be gone.

"Hello." Colby finally answered. By the wariness in his voice, he knew exactly who'd called.

"Is Elias dead?"

"What? No. Of course not."

"We heard the news. A cop died on a drug bust, and he won't answer the phone. Colby, don't lie to me. I need to know if he's okay."

"Vicki, no, I wouldn't lie to you. Hold on."

She heard low voices and the static of the radio. Was that Elias's voice? She couldn't be sure. It was too muffled. That son of a bitch. If he was sitting there, too afraid to get on the phone and deal with her himself...

She yelled into the phone. "Is Elias dead? Damn it, he'd better be dead if he won't answer his phone. He'd better be lying dead in the street with a crater blown in his skull to scare me like this. I've been calling him all day and then hear that a cop is dead and he won't answer his fucking phone?"

"Vicki, it's me. I'm fine."

Elias. She dropped her head against the fridge and sank farther into Jesse's embrace, letting him take all her weight. "I thought you were dead. I thought they killed you."

"I'm sorry, babe. I didn't know the news had broken already or I would have answered. I just didn't think."

"You didn't want to talk to *me*," she replied in a flat, dead voice. "Fine. I get it. You don't have the balls to talk to me. You don't love me enough to work things out. That's okay. I was wrong, I guess. I was wrong about everything."

He started to say something but she disconnected the call and let the phone drop to the floor. It hit so hard the back popped off and the battery skidded across the floor, but she left it. She didn't care.

Jesse tucked his face close to hers. "What can I do? How can I help?"

She straightened, squared her shoulders, lifted her chin, and grabbed a tissue to blow her nose. Then she smiled at him, although it was a weary one tinged in sadness. "Put those brownies in the oven for me?"

"You got it."

"Then we're going to watch every zombie movie known to man."

"Sign me up for that too." Jesse scraped the batter into the greased pan and slid the brownies into the oven. "I'm always up for a good zombie flick."

"Good is debatable, but I love them anyway."

He came to her, his hair loose about his face, his gorgeous eyes somber. Her heart hurt just looking at him, but it was a good pain. He was wearing his ratty old jeans again. If she checked his pockets, she'd probably find small bills crumbled up in each one, and the rest spread out in his bag, which she'd noticed at the door this morning. In case he had to make a run for it. She knew without checking that she'd find all the clothes she'd bought for him downstairs in the closet.

He'd gained back his normal weight, but his jeans still rode low on his hips, especially with his hands shoved down in the pockets. He didn't say anything, but she read his doubt in the way his shoulders hunched and he kept his eyes downcast. He still couldn't believe she hadn't kicked him out to bring Elias home.

She reached around him, sliding her hand around his waist and down into his jeans to grip his buttock, digging her fingers into his flesh like he...she...enjoyed the most. "You're mine, Jesse. Nobody is taking you away from me. Not even Elias."

At three a.m. Elias sat outside Vicki's apartment in his truck, took another swig of Jack straight from the bottle, and called himself a pussy. He'd been sitting out here drinking for half an hour, and still hadn't found the nerve to go up and see if she'd let him in. Oh, sure, he could use his key, but that would feel too much like sneaking.

Maybe she'd changed the locks. She'd been pissed enough to do something like that, and for good reason.

He'd never been so petty to hurt a woman he cared about like that before. Thinking about how scared she must have been to hear about a dead cop and then get his voicemail made him feel like dog crap. He's sworn to his first wife that he'd always answer the phone. Even if he was in the middle of handcuffing some dirtbag, he'd plant a knee in the perp's back and take her call. She'd still divorced his ass.

What the hell will Vicki do to me?

Rightfully so too. He deserved the biggest ass-chewing she'd ever thought about giving him. He'd left her. Again. He'd hurt her. Again. Then he'd scared ten years off her life. Now he sat out here too scared to go up and face the music.

No, that wasn't true. He'd always been able to deal with her temper. In fact, nothing turned him on more than watching her rip into him, teeth, fists, words, it didn't matter. He loved it.

No, what scared the shit out of him was the thought of finding her in bed with Jesse. Maybe this time they wouldn't be asleep. He'd catch them in the act and he'd...he'd...

What, blow the kid's brains out? She loved Jesse. It wasn't his fault. It wasn't even her fault. Elias saw the way she looked at the kid, because he looked at her the same way. He'd do anything to be with her, wouldn't he?

Even join them?

Yeah, that's what made his stomach churn uneasily. Whiskey burned a hole in his stomach. He just didn't know if he could do it. What it would entail. How would it feel to see her with another man, the passion on her face, and know it wasn't for him? That's what it came down to, wasn't it? His pride. His fear that maybe she secretly wanted Jesse more. Maybe he pleased her more. Hell, he hadn't even known that she might like the kinkier shit.

Maybe someday she'd decide she didn't really need Elias after all.

Much safer to walk now than to want and need her so bad and know he wasn't enough.

He reached for the keys to turn the engine on, but let his hand fall back into his lap. He'd sat here too long with the bottle to even think about driving. That's the last thing he needed. He could see the headlines now: *Drunk cop runs down helpless old lady in the street.*

He wasn't drunk, not by a long shot. Because if he were drunk, maybe he wouldn't care if she screamed the same way for Jesse that she did when *he* was inside her.

A flicker of movement drew his gaze up to the window. Her face, her hands pressed against the glass. Instinctively he scrunched back in his seat, but she couldn't see his truck, let alone him. He'd always been careful to park in the shadows, untouched by the streetlights when he came to stand watch outside her door.

She looked up and down the street and turned away. Warmth spread in his gut that absolutely nothing to do with whiskey. She'd been looking for him. Hoping that maybe he'd come, even though they'd such a horrible argument. Even though she'd hung up on him and refused to answer his calls the rest of the day. She had a good-looking, young cabana boy in her bed more than willing to do absolutely anything she asked.

Yet she was looking for me.

He got out of the truck and shut the door as quietly as possible. He still felt like a slinking hyena as he crept up the stairs and silently unlocked her door, but he held that vision of her at the window in his mind. All the lights were off but she'd left the television on. Blankets were tumbled about on the couch. She must have spent the day watching movies. Hopefully she hadn't been daydreaming about slicing him up like those killer zombies.

He kicked off his shoes and tiptoed toward her bedroom. The door was open. She wasn't trying to hide anything. She hadn't placed homemade tripwires or secretly moved any furniture into his path, hoping the crash would alert her of his approach. Still, he hesitated at the door, just to the side of the blackness within, gathering his courage. He didn't hear anything. No low moans, no sweet whispers, no thudding of flesh on flesh. No matter what he saw in her bed, he silently resolved not to leave. Not this time.

I'll take my punishment like a man.

Boldly, he stepped into her bedroom and stood in the dim moonlight leaking through the blinds on the window. Jesse was flat on his stomach, asleep, his face buried in Vicki's pillow.

Elias's pillow was twisted sideways, a dented, misshapen lump that looked like she'd been using it to beat somebody. But his side of the bed was empty.

He whipped his head around just in time to catch a glimpse of her flying out of the bathroom. She crashed into him and wrapped her arms so tightly he couldn't breathe. He didn't need to breathe. Not with her in his arms.

"Elias," she whispered in between fervent kisses over his face and throat. "Elias. I thought I'd lost you."

"I'm here, babe, and I'm not going anywhere this time."

She jerked open his pants. "Prove it."

Ah, his Vik, always the brash and bold one. He scooped her up in his arms and carried her to his side of the bed. He laid them both down as gently as possible, because the last thing he wanted right now was to deal with her other man.

Now that he had her beneath him, he could only stare down into her face, her large eyes, luminescent in the moonlight. "I'm sorry, babe. So sorry. I thought I could deal with it, no problem, but I was wrong."

"You need time. I understand." She unbuttoned his shirt and pushed her hands beneath to stroke his back, pulling him closer into the cradle of her thighs. "I'm asking a lot of you. Maybe too much."

"No. Not too much. Because..." He looked into her eyes, letting her see the depth of his need, how stark raving mad it had made him to think of losing her. "I love you, Vicki Connagher."

She smiled tremulously, but there was nothing hesitant about her hand slipping inside his pants as she worked his cock free. "Then make love to me, Detective Reyes."

He stole a sideways glance at the other man beside them. "I've never seen a street person sleep like he does. It's a miracle he lived long enough to find you, babe."

Jesse lifted his head and met his gaze warily, like a doe stepping into rush-hour traffic on the freeway. "You never sleep on the street, not really. But here..."

The kid's gaze said it all: *She makes me feel safe.*

Elias nodded. "Yeah, she does that to me too."

"*She*—" Vicki dug her nails into his back and squirmed against him, trying to get him to slide home. "Has no idea what you're talking about, but I'm pretty sure she needs you very badly."

In a low, small voice, Jesse asked, "Do you want me to leave?"

Elias glanced back at him and then down into Vicki's face. She didn't answer. She waited for his response. Yeah, he'd like to kick the kid out of her bed, house and life. But that wasn't happening, because she'd have a hole in her heart the same size as the hole she'd leave in Elias's heart if he lost her.

"No," he finally said in a rough voice. The tips of his ears burned so hot he was sure his entire body had burst into flame. "But I'm not into men, okay?"

"Okay." Jesse managed to make himself even smaller in the bed, withdrawing to the very edge. "I'm not either, when I have the choice."

Vicki wrapped her legs around Elias's waist and pressed her lips to his ear. "Thank you."

He thrust deep and closed his eyes, simply feeling the heat and warmth of her wrapped around him. This was home. Not the force, not his partner, not his dump of an apartment he'd called home for the last ten years.

Vicki made everything else in his life bearable. She brought light into the filth and horror he saw on the streets every single day. He could imagine all too well the foulness that Jesse had lived through to come home.

Home to her. To us.

Chapter Nineteen

Afraid to move and draw the cop's attention back to him, Jesse lay flat on his stomach and tried to ignore the uncomfortable throb of his erection smashed against the mattress. He did keep his head turned so he could watch. The cop hadn't forbidden watching.

For awhile, Elias simply lay on top of Vicki, giving her his full weight, pressing her deep enough into the mattress that it would have been really easy for Jesse to accidentally on purpose tumble against them. He gripped the fitted sheet harder, both to resist temptation and to give his hands something to do besides reach down and stroke himself. She hadn't told him what to do, whether he could enjoy her pleasure or not. Could he listen to her cries and not come? He didn't think so, but he was terrified of what the cop might do to him.

It was one thing to make love to her while Jesse watched. Elias surely wouldn't care to see him come all over her sheets.

Damn, the cop had big hands. He stroked those big palms up and down Vicki's arms, her sides, up her hip to shift her wider for him. She loved those hands too, arching and purring at his touch. Elias wasn't a big man, no bigger than Jesse in fact, but he carried himself like a giant. When he thrust deep, she arched her back and groaned, and Jesse had to bite down on his lip to keep from groaning with her. Elias shifted up on his knees slightly, giving himself better leverage, and he began to hammer inside her like he was determined to break her open and look for candy.

She raked her nails down his back hard enough Jesse could see the lines in the man's flesh. His own skin prickled, aching for her to do that to him. Maybe once the cop was more comfortable with him around, he could ask her to scratch him like that while the cop made love to her.

Elias let out a low chuckle and grabbed her wrists, tugging her arms over her head so she couldn't scratch him. Oh, damn, she must hate that and love it at the same time, because she snarled at him, fighting to get her hands free. It was all Jesse could do not to open his mouth and beg for her to hold him down like that.

Gripping her hands above her head with his left hand, Elias slipped his other hand down to squeeze her breast. Jesse could almost feel the hardness of her nipple, the tempting softness of her flesh. He wanted to suck and lick, first one and then the other, endlessly. He could worship her for hours that way. Better yet...

Elias's hand moved down between her thighs and Jesse had to bite his lip harder yet, but he couldn't entirely stifle his moan.

Both of their heads turned toward him, one set of eyes smoldering with passion, the other's dark with rising fury. Jesse could see the shimmering tension in her body. Even though he'd accidentally interrupted them, she was still close to coming. Looking at him wasn't helping, and she'd never forgive him if he ruined this make-up moment with Elias.

"No," she said, her voice ringing with command.

Jesse squeezed his eyes shut and nodded. Damn, damn, he had to hold it. Fire burned and licked in his groin, need rumbling closer to eruption, but he had to contain it.

"What the hell was that all about?" Elias asked.

"I told him not to come."

The cop's eyes flared wide and he let out a low rumbling chuckle that made Jesse burn to plant his razor between Elias's ribs. "Oh, yeah, I remember you telling me about that little arrangement. This is going to be fun, then." He sat back on his heels, kneeling between her thighs. "Roll over, babe."

For once, Vicki actually looked a little scared. "No, Elias, not that, really..."

"Come on, babe. Let's give him a damn good show." Suddenly magnanimous, he even managed to wink at Jesse. "You know he'll love it."

She shuddered and let out a delicious moan that made a drop of fluid leak from Jesse's aching cock. Without a word, she rolled over, rose up on her knees, and buried her face in the crook of her arm.

Elias slid back inside, calm and easy. Confused, Jesse watched, braced for fireworks but nothing happened. What did she have against basic doggie-style?

Tugging her hips back farther, Elias subtly changed his thrust, pushing up higher, lifting her despite the resistance of his grip on her thighs. She tossed her head, moaning into her arm, and Jesse leaned closer, straining to see in the darkness.

Lowering his chest against her back, Elias gave her more weight, beginning to hold her down. Penning her. "Come on, Vik. I know you want to buck. Don't make me dig my spurs into you."

She said something that was muffled into the pillow. Or maybe she cursed. "Don't do this to him. It's not fair. You can be a cruel bastard, Reyes."

The cop smiled and winked at Jesse again, smugness and yeah, a bit of edgy cruelty shadowing his face. He gave her a long, deep thrust that made her claw the mattress.

"Elias, God, please."

"Feel me deep, babe. Feel me so deep inside that you can taste me." He thrust again, a sinuous, lifting drive that made her groan rise to a howl. "There's that spot you like so much. You love to feel me there, don't you, babe? Let's see if I can touch it again."

He dropped more of his weight against her, using his left forearm to trap her upper body, his hand fisted in her hair. She stared across the expanse of the mattress at Jesse. He had a moment to see the heat in her eyes, and then Elias slammed deep again and her eyes rolled back. Her mouth fell open, her hands tearing at the sheets, her voice rising as the climax went on and on. Elias pushed deeper, not even thrusting, but stroking deep inside. She erupted, flailing in the throes of her climax.

Jesse couldn't watch. Listening was bad enough. His whole body hurt with the need to simply explode, but she'd told him no. In agony, he felt like flailing and wailing right along with her. God above, he'd never heard that sound come from her lips before. She screamed like Elias was killing her. She was furious, crazed, and so far gone with passion that it was the most glorious, beautiful sound Jesse had ever heard in his entire life. She pleaded, begged, cursed at Elias to stop, and he just laughed and did it again.

And again. Perhaps there was a bit of sadist in the cop after all.

When Elias finally roared out his own release, Jesse was as sweaty and sore as if he'd run a marathon. Every muscle in his body ached from fighting back his own release. If she even looked at him, he'd probably explode, the cop and her order be damned.

Draped on top of her, Elias brushed damp hair from her face and kissed her neck tenderly. "You okay, babe?" She groaned wretchedly, making him laugh. "That good, huh. How about you show me what you like to do with your boy for round two."

Jesse stiffened from head to foot, his ears ringing. He squeezed his eyes and mouth shut, refusing to say a word or give her any indication how badly he wanted her to do anything to him. Anything at all. Let the cop watch. Let him beat him within an inch of his life, he didn't care, as long as she gave him release.

The bed dipped as she rolled to the middle of it. It was all he could do not to arch his back and try to drill a hole through the mattress with his cock.

"Are you sure?"

Yes, yes, please, Jesse babbled in his mind. He was going to suffocate himself on this pillow, trying to keep from blurting out her name.

"I have something in mind."

Jesse jolted like someone had dumped ice-cold water on him. What the hell did that mean?

"If you don't have anything handy to tie him up, I'll offer my handcuffs."

This time Jesse whimpered and he didn't care who heard.

Vicki checked the scarf from her dress around Jesse's wrists one last time. He was breathing so fast she was afraid he'd hyperventilate. "Are you sure you're okay?"

"Please, Vicki, hurry. I hurt so bad. I can't stand it."

She stole a glance at Elias, still unsure of his motives. He lay on his side watching her. Yesterday, he'd walked out on her. Now he wanted her tie her cabana boy up and torment him. While Elias watched. After they'd just...

Her face caught fire at the memory. When he held her down like that and went so deep he bumped her cervix, she always went nuts. Mama had told her to make him grovel, but she really had no idea how to bring Elias to his knees while she was playing with another man. She brushed damp hair off Jesse's forehead and he lifted his face, twisting up to get her fingers into his mouth.

He sucked her fingers, stroking frantically with his tongue, and she let her eyes flutter shut. This was all she needed to worry about. Pleasing him while pleasing herself, and indirectly, pleasing Elias too. She opened her eyes and checked his reaction. His eyes were dark, locked on her, but he wasn't tense or angry. Instead, his lips were parted and she could hear his breathing. He might not be comfortable with their situation yet, but he was turned on.

Let's see how far he'll let me go.

She pulled her fingers out of Jesse's mouth and bent down to kiss him. He raised his head off the pillow eagerly, inhaling her lips like a dying man. She threaded her fingers through his hair and pulled his head back down to the bed. He breathed hard, his eyes blazing.

"What do you want?"

"Anything. Everything. Just don't touch me down south until you're absolutely ready to lose me."

She stroked her palms in slow, gentle circles across his chest. He didn't really react much until she let her fingernails rake lightly over his skin. Especially his nipples. He hissed beneath his breath and arched his back, pushing harder so she dug into his skin. "Yes, please, harder, Vicki. I saw what you did to his back. I'd love that."

Leaning over him, she pressed her fingernails harder, deliberately leaving furrows in his skin as he'd asked. "Of course, I should kiss the sting away."

He groaned in agreement.

She didn't kiss those scratches, though. She licked them with long swipes of her tongue. He shifted beneath her, silently asking for her mouth on his nipples. Teasingly, she drew wet circles around them, ignoring his pleading cries. He twisted his hands, tugging at the scarves, and his legs shifted restlessly against the sheets. When he managed to brush up against her, he groaned and lifted his leg higher, redoubling his efforts to get her closer.

"Guess you should have tied his ankles up too, babe." Elias said it like a joke, but the low, ragged timbre of his voice thrummed her spine. "Maybe you should sit on those legs to hold him still."

"Did you hear him, Jesse?" She purred against his chest, pausing to scrape her teeth across his left nipple. "If you promise to lie still, I'll do it. I'll sit on your knees. But you can't move and make me touch you by accident before I'm ready."

"Okay." He panted, dragging his legs together. "I'll be good."

"Not his knees." Elias moved closer too, his gaze intent. "You'll need to be higher."

"Okay," she said slowly, unsure what he wanted. She'd assumed he wouldn't want to be involved at the same time.

When she settled herself across Jesse's thighs, he shuddered beneath her. "Oh, God, you're so wet. I wish you would rub yourself all over me."

It was a mistake to close her eyes, because that made it easier for her to imagine sliding up his body, smearing him with her desire. Or she could make him lick her while he was tied and helpless. He'd love it.

I'd love it, too, she admitted to herself. *But would Elias?*

She felt him behind her. She froze, waiting to see what he'd do. He, too, straddled the other man's legs, pressing close enough to her that she could feel his returned erection brushing the small of her back. He didn't touch Jesse, exactly, but he was definitely closer to the danger zone than Vicki had ever thought he'd get.

"Someday," Jesse gasped out, "I'd love you to sit on my face while he takes you from behind again. I'd drown in you and die a happy man."

Her ears roared and she swayed slightly. Elias steadied her by cupping her shoulders, but the warm moist heat of his breath at her ear did little to calm the sudden flood of desire. "Would you like that, Vik?"

Her body was on fire, crisped and burned beyond recognition, but she managed to nod. She rose on up on her knees instead of sitting on Jesse's thighs and pressed back against Elias. His heat against her back brought her body back to the edge of a screaming, clawing climax.

"Maybe some other night. Right now, I need to face my worst fear. I need to see you take him all the way. Take him inside your body and ride him to climax." He smoothed his right hand down the curve of her buttock and dipped his fingers in the desire that slickened her folds. "Ah, babe, I'm a selfish bastard. I'm going to have to touch you while you do it. I can't bear to know he's inside you if I'm not touching you too."

He was trying so hard. If he'd made a snide remark about his jealousy, she would have wanted to punch him, but he was being too honest for her temper to even think about coming forward. Elias had made himself vulnerable. He was willingly accepting a blow to his pride to accommodate her wishes.

He let out a husky laugh against her ear and his fingers roamed higher along the valley between her buttocks. He probed, ever so gently. She stiffened, but her entire body flooded with heat, a tell-tale trickle slipping down her thigh. They'd never played with anal before.

But then again, she'd never had another man in her bed, either.

"Trust me, babe. I won't go all the way this time. I don't want to hurt you. I just want you to think about it. Think about me coming inside you at the same time. Jesse, you're going to have to make this good for her. Make it last."

Jesse's breathing was labored. "I'll try."

"Take him," Elias growled in her ear. "But your ass is mine."

It was incredibly easy to rise up and slide over Jesse. It wasn't easy to keep from throwing her head back and letting loose like a bucking bronco. So good. Elias hot against her back, Jesse moaning and shaking beneath her. *Another dream come true.*

Elias's breath came hot and heavy against her ear. His other hand gripped her breast, holding her close to him. He rocked his body with hers, guiding her in a slow rolling ride, pushing her down on the other man, even while he pushed his finger deeper into her.

So full. She couldn't stand it. Pressure built with each incremental thrust. She couldn't stop thinking about his cock sliding into her. Surely he'd be too big. His finger alone was too much.

She cried out, instinctively trying to withdraw, but pulling away from him only put her in harder contact with Jesse. She ground her hips against him, seeking relief, and suddenly he was the one bucking, his back rising off the mattress, his hips thrusting up, hard, driving Elias deeper, and she lost it. Stars detonated in her head. Elias held her, his body rock-hard and steady against her. Her protector. Always at her back.

She was falling again, the world simply tumbling away, but he caught her. He tucked her tightly against him, drawing her into the shelter of his arms with his body curled against her back. Eventually, their breathing steadied, enough for her to realize that Jesse lay shivering beside her, his hands still bound to the headboard.

Guilt made her eyes burn. How long had she left him like that? She rose up and tugged on the scarf, struggling to get the tightened knots out. Not the smartest choice. She should have listened to Shiloh weeks ago. The scarf had bitten into his skin.

"That was incredible," he whispered, struggling to keep his eyes open. "You can tie me up any time you want, Vicki. Especially if that's the outcome."

"I shouldn't have used the silk. I'm sorry, Jesse. Can you still feel your fingers?"

She finally got it loosened enough for him to pull his hands free. Shaking his hands, he grinned up at her. "I'm good, but I won't be opposed to handcuffs next time."

Next time. She suddenly couldn't meet either man's gaze. Could Elias do it again? Or would he just walk out one day, never to return?

"Why don't you go take a shower," Elias suggested to Jesse. Without a word, the younger man slid out of her bed. Even in the darkness with another man lying behind her, she couldn't tear her gaze away from his ass. Her own backside burned, remembering the stretching pressure of Elias filling her up.

"Your ass is prettier than his," Elias whispered in her ear, drawing her back against him. "I don't feel anything when I look at him, until I look at you and see the heat in your eyes."

"Does it bother you?"

"I thought it would." He admitted, dropping his chin to her shoulder. "I thought..." He swallowed hard. "I thought you might want him more than me. That it'd be different between us now."

"Elias—" Her voice broke.

"Hear me out, babe. It is different now. I didn't think it possible to improve on our sex life, but it's better. Touching you like that... Damn, Vicki, it was so hot I came without even needing to be inside you. It's going to get even better as we get more comfortable with each other. I see how much you want him, and it's okay. It's okay because you still look at me and want me too."

She rolled over in his arms so she could see his face. She stroked her fingers over his brow, the grim line of his jaw. "I'll always want you."

His lips quirked, giving a nudge with his hips that showed her somebody was hard yet again. "Prove it."

She pushed him flat on his back. "It'll be my pleasure."

Chapter Twenty

The kitchen was dark except for the light radiating out of the fridge as she scrounged for something to eat. After such a rousing night, she needed some protein after all those brownies.

"I made something for you," Jesse said in that shy way that made her want to push him up against a wall and sink her teeth into his full bottom lip. He offered a heavy, thick sheet of paper.

"Turn on the light."

He did so, illuminating an ornate tree spreading across the page. Long, curling branches filled the sky, dotted with blue-green leaves and curls. The trunk was a deep, rich blood red, solid but gently curving in feminine hourglass. The base of the tree spread out into dark, thick roots reaching deep into the soil.

The colors were bright and vivid, not his usual chalks. Turquoise, red, black. "My colors!"

He grinned and reached across her shoulder to trail his finger along the tree's trunk. "This is you."

She cocked her head and she could make out her name written in the swirling bark. Tiny, detailed, elegantly curved letters became part of the pattern. His name floated in the leaves that matched the color of his eyes. Elias was dark, earthy, his name written in the soil and the foundation of the tree.

"You connect us. You're the trunk holding everything together. Without you, the leaves will dry up and crumble away."

Her throat ached. "Yet without the roots, the tree can't live either."

"Exactly."

"Thank you." She pulled him into her arms and brushed her lips against his. "It's perfect. I'm going to get it framed and hang it over the mantle." Staring into his eyes, she whispered, "I'm going to ask Elias something very important tonight."

Jesse let his breath out in a long exhale, as though preparing for the worst. "Okay."

"You know how much you mean to me, don't you?"

He smiled but his bottom lip trembled. "I'm yours to take, if you want me."

"You know I do. In fact, I want to keep you forever. If you want to stay with me, that is."

He blinked at her and opened his mouth, but no words came out.

"I love you, Jesse, and I want you to always be here, but I love Elias too. I don't want you to feel like a hand-me-down, or like I might ever change my mind and kick you out some day. I'd never do that, okay? You're part of my family now, so I want to give you something that is special, so that you know..."

"That I'm home? I already know that, Vicki. Even if you marry Elias, there's no place I'd rather be than with you."

She reached into her purse and pulled out the flat velvet box that Victor had helped her pick out. Her fingers trembled as much as her voice. "This isn't something I ever imagined doing, let alone offering to anyone, before I met you."

Holding the box in front of her, she flipped it open to reveal the collar inside. On a heavy, masculine platinum chain, turquoise sapphires the same color as Jesse's eyes formed the elaborate V of her label.

He stared at the jewelry, his eyes going wider and wider, but he barely breathed. She couldn't tell if he liked the idea or not. They'd never talked about the significance of a collar, *her* collar, because she'd never known herself. Maybe she'd guessed absolutely wrong. "If you don't like it..."

"Vicki," he breathed out her name like a prayer. Finally, he raised his gaze to hers, and his eyes shone brighter than the stones. "You got this for me?"

"Only for you. I want you to know that you belong with me, as long as you choose to stay."

He stepped closer so he could press his forehead to hers. "I never dared dream that you'd want me, let alone that you'd understand the rest. I'd love to wear your collar, Vicki. Whenever and however you want me, I'm yours."

She slipped the box back into her purse so she could hug him close. "I thought we could go somewhere, just you and me. Like a ceremony or something. Would you like that?"

"Our park," he whispered. "Where you first found me."

"You've got it."

"Hey, do you have anything to eat in here?" Elias strode in still wet from the shower and as naked as a jaybird. "I thought I smelled chocolate when I came in. I'm starving. Hey, that reminds me, Jesse. Are you free for another poker game this week? Colby's not the new guy on the force anymore, and we're breaking in the newest recruit. I swear no one will try to bust your face this time, unless you win too much."

"Sure thing." Jesse grinned, his relief and happiness at being included twisting her heart in a very good way. "You know it's a really good game when someone bleeds."

Elias saw the half-devoured pan of brownies still out on the stove and moved to dive right in, but she smacked the back of his hand.

"Ouch! What the hell was that for?"

"Those are my pity-party brownies. The ones I made because I was heartbroken and lonely. You can't eat them."

"Aw, babe, come on. I already apologized." He reached around her, sinking his fingers into the pan, but she shoved him aside before he could get more than a bite of the gooey batter. She hated dry, overcooked brownies. They'd eaten her brownies with a spoon. "We've had make-up sex, more sex, even shower sex. This man needs sustenance. He needs brownies!"

"Not yet. I've got something to say to you." She planted her hands on her hips and gave him her most determined courtroom glare. "I want a ring."

"Sure, babe." He laughed and reached for the pan again, but she punched him hard enough in the solar plexus that he grunted and took a step back.

"Not just any ring. An engagement ring. If you want me."

He narrowed his eyes and gave her his own belligerent, bad-cop glare. "I think I just proved pretty damn well that I want you, Vik."

"You did." She kept her voice pleasant and she smiled, the wide, toothy one that always made him blanch. "But if you want to prove it ever again, Detective Reyes, then I want a ring. I want to be your wife. I want you to answer your phone every single time I call you. I want you to come home every single night and eat all my brownies without me wondering if you're ever going to come home again."

He jerked his chin at the other man hovering off to the side. "What about him?"

She glanced at Jesse and gave him the same formidable smile. The difference with him: his knees went weak and his eyes smoldered like molten jewels. "I'm going to buy him a ring as proof of my solemn promise and commitment that he will always have a place in my house, my heart and my bed."

Elias took a growling, threatening step closer. "So I get to give you my name and he gets everything else?"

"No, *babe*," she drawled, lifting a handful of gooey chocolate from the pan. "You get my name, my house, my bed and my heart. I'll even give you my brownies." She reached out and wrapped her chocolate-covered hand around his cock. "If you let me eat some off you at the same time."

With a wicked grin, Jesse headed for the shower, leaving Elias to suffer her brownie punishment alone.

He groaned and leaned back against the counter. Reaching around him with her free hand, she scooped up more brownies, letting him eat off her fingers.

"You make the best brownies in the world. Vicki Connagher, will you do me the honor of becoming my wife?"

"Yes," she whispered, smearing his lips with chocolate. Then she went to her knees before him. She licked just the tip of him and he trembled, gripping the counter like it was the only thing holding him up.

"Uh, babe? I think I'm the one who's supposed to be on their knees for this question."

She smiled up at him. "You will be. Soon." She licked him again and the counter creaked in sympathy. "I'm going to make you grovel."

Before she got back to the pan for another brownie, he did.

About the Author

Joely always has her nose buried in a book, especially one with mythology, fairy tales and romance. She, her husband and their three monsters live in Missouri. By day, she's a computer programmer with a Masters of Science degree in Mathematics. When night falls, she bespells the monsters so she can write. Read more about her current projects on her website, http://joelysueburkhart.com.

Every deal has a loophole.

Restraining the Receptionist
© 2011 Juniper Bell
...the Receptionist, Book 2

Dana Arthur's new job with the firm of Cowell & Dirk is going well. Translation: the occasionally kinky ménage with her two bosses, Ethan and Simon, has been several months of politically incorrect bliss.

Except the relationship feels unbalanced. While Ethan is the undisputed master, the partners' iron-clad agreement stipulates that Simon must be present as she performs her "duties". And she senses there's a subtle, powerful tug-of-war developing for more than just her body.

Simon had agreed to share the firm's fiery, sensually daring receptionist...to a point. With Simon out of town, Ethan plans a feast of erotic temptations designed to have Dana begging him to break the deal. He didn't realize his heart would be a casualty.

Once she surrenders to his wicked demands, Dana realizes there's no going back. It's time for a three-way renegotiation... this time, all or nothing.

Warning: NSFW!! Do Not Try This at Your Job. Contains highly inappropriate workplace behavior including m/f/m, m/m, bondage, creative use of office space and a high-stakes trip to Atlantic City.

Available now in ebook from Samhain Publishing.

SAMHAIN
PUBLISHING

It's all about the story...

Romance

HORROR

www.samhainpublishing.com

CPSIA information can be obtained at www.ICGtesting.com
Printed in the USA
BVOW020837070313

314963BV00006B/20/P